The Songs of Michael Flanders and Donald Swann

With a Foreword by Donald Swann

ST MARTIN'S PRESS · NEW YORK

All inquiries about performing rights in these numbers should be addressed to
Lister Welch Ltd, 10/12 Cork Street, London W1

The publishers gratefully acknowledge the following for their kind permission to
reproduce copyright drawings in this book: The Estate of H. M. Bateman (p. 72);
Mrs Kenneth Bird (p. 93); Mrs Gerald Hoffnung (p. 103, from *The Hoffnung
Symphony Orchestra*, Dobson Books); Osbert Lancaster (p. 78, from *Cowardy
Custard*, William Heinemann Ltd); the Trustees of the Estate of David Low and the
London *Evening Standard* (pp. 114-5); Peter Owen Ltd, London (p. 75, from
Gerald Scarfe's People); *Punch* (pp. 11, 17, 29, 41, 70, 99 and 124).
Drawing by Edward Burra (p. 83, from *ABC of the Theatre* by Humbert Wolfe).
The drawings by ffolkes (pp. 152-218), Hewison (p.144) and Ionicus (p.126)
were commissioned for this volume.
The publishers also wish to thank Chappells for permission to reproduce the
following numbers appearing in their *Flanders and Swann Song Book*: Hippopo-
tamus, Rhinoceros, Elephant, Whale, Warthog; and Samuel French for permission
to reproduce the following numbers from their book *Airs On A Shoestring &
Penny Plain*: Guide to Britten, Design for Living, Last of the Line, Budget Song,
Ballad for the Rich.

Contents

Foreword

The idea of writing a foreword to this selection of the songs that Michael Flanders and I wrote seems an easier task than that of making up the book. Many noble fiends of work have been involved: Carlo Ardito of St George's Press, who helpfully insisted and assisted, Claudia Flanders who valiantly selected and edited the lyrics, and William Blezard who collaborated with Michael Hatwell in sorting out my musical scribbles and made many of my unplayables playable . . . Alas, far behind them all is one who ought to be somewhere in the van, the rascal Donald—billed as Composer! So starts my meditation upon the existence of this book.

It all stems from the night of 31 December 1956, when Michael and I suddenly became converts to a personal presentation of our songs on stage: when *At the Drop of a Hat* hit us like a bolt from the blue, in the New Lindsey Theatre, Notting Hill Gate, seating just over 200. (It is now a road, not a brick left.) Ever since we started work in the theatre in 1949 and 1950, Max Adrian, Ian Wallace, Rose Hill and many other fine revue artists had been interpreting our songs, immaculately accompanied by John Pritchett, Betty Robb, Bill Blezard and others. Some of these songs are indeed in this book: 'Last of the Line' and 'Guide to Britten', for instance, are from *Airs on a Shoestring*, a revue which ran at the Royal Court Theatre from 1953 to 1955. Anyone who asked for these songs was referred to our loyal publishers, Chappells, who had by then printed half a dozen, including *Hippopotamus* and a few other animals, secure in the hands of Ian Wallace, while amateur dramatic enthusiasts applied to Samuel French, the theatrical publishers who had given the light of print, with full stage directions, to a dozen songs from *Airs on a Shoestring* and earlier revues to which we had contributed. Beyond this, Michael and I had forgotten, literally and definitely, that there was such a thing as publication.

I well recall the upswing to that Opening Night at the New Lindsey: we were playing over the songs we had chosen in the studio at 1A Scarsdale Villas (where Michael had a 'bite out of the pavement', so goes the introduction to the 'Gnu' song, so as to be able to wheel himself in) to Frederick Piffard, the only theatre manager who was ever attacked by a lion—or was it a tiger?—and survived to return to Show Business with success, thank God. We said we would like the New Lindsey for two weeks.

'Nice songs,' said Freddie Piffard, 'but who's in it?'

'Us,' we said timidly.

'Well, you pay the rent,' he said, 'it's up to you.'

Our audience that New Year's Eve was the Dartington Hall Summer School of Music mailing list, which we had borrowed from John Amis; Dartington was where we had tried out the songs in the past summer. And others turned up, thanks to our then Press Officer, Pat Orr-Ewing, who had written to all the theatre critics blithely assuming that no one else would open a show on New Year's Eve. In fact I don't think anyone else did, and they came.

When after two weeks we obviously seemed like a hit, the Blow Fell: 'Come into the Fortune Theatre!' We turned it down unanimously. It seemed to spell the end of Michael's radio career (he had by that time done at least a thousand broadcasts) and the end of Swann as composer for revues, as backroom boy writing music for Laurier Lister's shows and at other parts of the day going all lyrical, writing intellectual love-songs in Greek . . . But Michael and I had some 48 to 72 hours of no sleep—and we accepted. We were HAT performers, and the songs were converted to being stage items, altering nightly for each audience, based often on a simple motif but made more complex all the time by the stops, pauses, bending of tempo, asides, and—where they came—by the laughs of the audience, those real 'stops' where one draws breath and thinks again.

At the beginning of *At the Drop of a Hat* we were totally aural—singing the songs ourselves with no prompt script, no score. It was a long-lasting joke of Michael's that while he had to know my music by heart, *I* always required the lyrics on my stand! Our stage manager, as some may recall, was the girl who brought on the Hat for 'Madeira M'dear' . . . The first Hat girl was Judith Jackson, who now writes about cars for the Sunday papers, and the gorgeous blonde at the Fortune Theatre was Carole Anne Aylett. The Hat-cum-A.S.M. at the Haymarket several years later actually saw the Resident Ghost of the theatre, Mr Buckstone, standing near Michael in the wings. Michael felt this blessing on his work very warmly and the story is now quoted in most spooky books on London.

I should stick to the point, and in a foolish way I may have made it: it is that *At the Drop of a Hat* and its successor became a show, and the songs left the page for a time, coming alive up there on the boards. So-called composer that I was, I never wrote any of them down: Michael improvised when he felt like it and otherwise kept to the tramline of patter that he had moved along on previous nights and knew was working. He was constantly improving and altering; I varied the accompaniments, and laughed anew as the jokes grew.

From the beginning, Michael and I felt drawn to the same musical styles. Our tastes were classical, ballad, music hall and folk song—intermingled. So 'Bedstead Men', for instance, matches up to an old English ballad; in the lyric one feels Michael was looking back to his school days in Sussex and Kent, and to walks on the downs at Lancing College near Shoreham, where we were both evacuated during the war from Westminster School. Music Hall influence is obvious in 'Transport of Delight' but as usual we juggled with the traditional style to get variations. Classical tastes come out in 'Ill Wind', borrowed rather than stolen from Mozart for use in Mike's baritonal range; also in 'Guide to Britten', in which all who saw Max Adrian will never forget his special brilliance as the 'conductor'. As for 'All Gall', 'The Budget' and the 'Song of the Weather', these are either actual or parodied folk songs. Michael's affection for place names, and the English villages themselves, emerges in 'Slow Train', and this is linked to his love of *objects* which I reckon was at least as strong as that of personified animals, in which vein he liked to trace his 'lineage' back as far as Aesop. This book includes several such 'object' songs, not only about Slow Trains but also the Last Tram in London and the London Omnibus, and about ever-ubiquitous Pillar Boxes and Bedsteads in Ponds.

We hope in this book to present you with the 'song element' out of what I like to call the 'serpentine jigsaw' of our show, where Michael used to set songs up obliquely, as for example in his hilarious telling of a story about air travel, suddenly to surprise his audience with the gentle and melodic 'Slow Train'. This jigsaw pattern we had learned as we wrote for Laurier Lister's revues, in which surprise and the unknown were always the essence. Performing on stage we added—like other revue artists—more surprises, to amuse ourselves and the audience too. So in the end nothing was final, only the experience of the show itself. Our newer HAT songs were not for issue, we said, they were part of our act.

The idea of a book—this book—came to life in 1975 and 1976, and still many songs had remained un-notated. But not all: a handful of them had been prepared for the Chappells *Michael Flanders and Donald Swann Song Book*. An odd one, 'Armadillo', had been originally written out for Sir Don Bradman, who felt he needed it in Australia! So most of the music remained only in my mind, till Carlo Ardito turned up on my doorstep suddenly and said, 'Donald, if you want the book, where is the music?'

Actually, when I think back to the later HAT performances, I remember that I was beginning to have rebellious thoughts: why, I thought, could not *my* music, and I was brought up in a family where actual bits of music, the paper stuff itself, lay in abundance on the piano, why could not my music, I repeated to myself, be published and available? 'Fiddlesticks,' said Michael, or words to that effect. 'You haven't got the point: our performances can't be written down, and if the complexities of the music and the word-juggling were taken out, it wouldn't look or sound like much anyhow . . . Be glad that we are lucky enough to have our pretty small group of songs working, on stage. Each song is a particle of a show. And there are just (and as it turned out, would only be) two HATs'. As a consolation to myself I wrote 'Two Moods for Tuba' which is, I gather, now known by tuba players, thanks to the Chamber Music Library of Tenafly, New Jersey—but I still felt baulked. And I did go on to compose music for myself and others in a variety of veins. (I suppose there was some small satisfaction to be gained from sending Michael, later on, the Catalogue of my Published Music and indeed from receiving from him and Joseph Horovitz their admirable *Captain Noah and His Floating Zoo*—in print!)

The musical team and I have had to take some hard decisions about the music in this book: sometimes we've been able to print it just as I used to play it—'Misalliance', 'Armadillo', 'The Whale (Mopy Dick)', 'The Lord Chamberlain's Regulations', 'The Sloth' and some others. I have felt that it would not be easy to compromise a note, or leave out a key change, as these songs had been thus composed and fixed in my imagination . . . But with another group—'In the Bath', 'Ostrich', 'Spider'—it was possible to leave them *almost* as we conceived and sang them, but to imagine adaptations to make them easier. And some songs are part of the jigsaw group, where total notation is impossible, such as 'Wompom': on the record this is *prestissimo*, with noises made by mouth (note how the King's Singers manage them), but in the new notation it's still a complete performable version. Happily these songs are nearly all thus, though here and there, as in 'Motor Perpetuo', we have given the main melody only, the chorus. Finally there is the group which we have tried to make as acceptable as possible for the clever-but-casual pianist: 'Twice Shy', 'Song of the Weather', 'Design for Living' are among these, uncomplicated folk or revue-style melodies, where the top line is in the right hand of the piano, enabling even a learner pianist to have a go. And the lyrics are always there in full.

I suppose I could prowl on, but why? Whoever secures this book and is musically minded will see what I mean, from any song at which he happens to open. And now we have illustrations, too, as the old revues had back-cloths: how lovely it is to join words and music to cartoons, especially when so many are by *Punch*'s most distinguished artists, not forgetting one by Gerard Hoffnung, who occasioned Michael's threat of a Tuba at the end of 'Ill Wind' . . . God bless also Ronald Searle, who has followed his original *Punch* cartoon of us at our opening all those years ago, which was so often used later on programmes, with a new drawing for the jacket.

Shall I offer some technical Notes on the Notes? 'Ill Wind' originated in Michael's captivation with the famous Rondo sections of the 4th Mozart Horn Concerto. I swear the gramophone record he used was several revolutions too fast, but Michael was a master of fast singing, so I got out the orchestral part as usually printed, and played it as writ. For this effort—playing 'good' classical music—I sprained my wrist and had writer's cramp for nine months! So I compromised: I made some of the reiterated orchestral chords into Alberti-style arpeggios, and no one noticed, least of all Mozart. People were, after all, listening to Michael's 'horn . . . gorn' rhymes, and to his own comic vocal cadenza. So we have printed Mozart with roulades—just that bit easier. This simplification was produced by the organist-pianist and singer, Roger Cleverdon.

'The Slow Train' is in 6/8 time; for years I imagined it in 4/4, but I was never sure of the tempo in *At the Drop of Another Hat*, as I found I had to vary the accompaniment to catch up with our 'train' melody. It took the King's Singers, as recently as January 1977, to clarify, by the use of six voices, that the 'train' runs in 6/8 and only as I heard them did the riddle find an answer, and the train rolled for the first time evenly over its sleepers.

'Song of Patriotic Prejudice' was a jigsaw number, full of curious bits and pieces in the show and on the record; but peering at it during editing, I decided it is best offered in a simple form with regular verses and refrains, whereupon it turns into a severely needed new English National Song to which Michael referred in introducing it: after all, the English, the English, the English are best! (Please read the lyric at once for the ironical overtones . . .)

Even the easy-going Hippo acquired his complexities, and I would relish singing it in Russian as I used to do. The Russian is not here, though above my desk are Hippos in some eighteen languages, garnered over the years. (Perhaps some day Claudia and I will publish 'The Obscurities of Flanders and Swann'?)

Finally, I have put in metronome marks: I had a fetish about these, and about accurate tempi, for years and years. They give an idea of the speeds I have in mind. However, performers may wish to reinterpret speed as well as idiom—as long as 'The Sloth' is not taken *molto agitato* nor 'Ill Wind' as a dirge!

In fact this book liberates everyone from the known performances, though the records are five, and they're listed somewhere in this book. The 'live', and to most folk singers 'true' music is the main source: that is how the thing sounds and is—or sounded and was.

Claudia Flanders and I decided that the songs must now be made available. They can be taken from here, from these pages, and can grow again in your, the player's hands, with your or another's voice. Our Founder Father, Laurier Lister, has a dream that one day the live element of some of these and other songs might be restored on stage: possibly a new cast of actors may make the dream come true. But through this book we welcome *your* new performances and new interpretations; the change has now come, and Michael would approve. Each singer will do what he pleases, and so he should. The E.M.I. records keep the old two-man pattern alive, yet readers and players may find our adaptations for piano and voice a help toward recapturing an idiom that is an amalgam of music, words *and* performance.

Whilst there is no room in this foreword to describe our tours abroad and other adventures, the pioneering efforts of Alexander Cohen to get us to America deserve special mention.

Well, I've looked backward enough for a foreword, and we've put the music down. Here is a book of 41 songs, to which Chappells and Samuel French have graciously lent their contributions.

Some of my cogitations here could legitimately precede a published script of, say, a radio drama. And many may query the validity of my comments. Commenting on my own songs gives me no credentials of a Pope Ex-piano-stool-Cathedra. The writer was not me, verbose and abstract—it was the other one, the bluff bearded one, the one with the chiselled words and the laconic wit, who never wasted a comma, who typed clearly and thought lucidly. I shall always and forever miss my wonderful colleague, my friend Michael, who should be writing this introduction to the book of our songs. And ex his wheel-chair cathedra he would have made a scintillating job of it.

DONALD SWANN

In the Bath

Oh, I find much simple pleasure when I've had a tiring day
In the bath, in the bath!
Where the noise of gentle sponging seems to blend with my top A
In the bath, in the bath!
To the skirl of pipes vibrating in the boiler room below,
I sing a pot-pourri of all the songs I used to know,
And the water thunders in and gurgles down the overflow
In the bath, in the bath!

Then the loathing for my fellows rises steaming from my brain
In the bath, in the bath!
And condenseth to the Milk of Human Kindness once again
In the bath, in the bath!
Oh, the tingling of the scrubbing brush, the flannel's soft caress!
To wield a lordly loofah is a joy I can't express.
How truly it is spoken, one is next to Godliness
In the bath, in the bath!

Then there comes that dreadful moment when the water's running cold
In the bath, in the bath!
When the soap is lost forever and one's feeling tired and old
In the bath, in the bath!
It's time to pull the plug out, time to mop the bathroom floor.
The towel is in the cupboard, and the cupboard is next door!
It's started running hot! Let's have another hour or more
In the bath, in the bath!

I can see the one salvation of the poor old human race
In the bath, in the bath!
Let the nations of the world all meet together face to face
In the bath, in the bath!
One with Kissinger, Kosygin and all those other chaps,
Sadat and Chairman Mao, then we'll have some peace perhaps—
Provided Harold Wilson gets the end without the taps
In the bath, in the bath!

Warmly flowing ♩ = 104

1. Oh, I find much sim-ple plea-sure when I've
(2.) loa-thing for my fel-lows ri - ses
(3.) see the one sal-va-tion of the

had a tir - ing day
stea-ming from my brain
poor old hu - man race
In the bath, in the bath! Where the
And con-
Let the

noise of gen-tle spon-ging seems to blend with my top A In the bath, in the
-den-seth to the Milk of Hu - man Kind-ness once a - gain In the bath, la-la-la-la-la-la, in the
na - tions of the world all meet to - ge - ther face to face In the bath, in the

bath! To the skirl of pipes vi - bra-ting in the boi - ler room be - low I
bath! Oh, the ting-ling of the scrubbing brush, the flan-nel's soft ca - ress! To
bath! One with Kis-sing - er, Ko - sy - gin and all those o - ther chaps, Sa -

13

sing a pot-pour-ri of all the songs I used to know, And the wa-ter thun-ders in and gur-gles

wield a lord-ly loo-fah is a joy I can't ex-press. How tru-ly it is spo-ken, one is

-dat and Chairman Mao, then we'll have some peace per-haps — Pro-vi-ded Ha-rold Wil-son gets the

down the o - ver-flow } In the bath, in the bath! 2.Then the bath.

next to God - li-ness }

moody

A bit mournful

3.Then there comes that dread-ful mo-ment when the wa-ter's run-ning cold In the

bath, in the bath! When the soap is lost for-ev-er and one's feel-ing tired and old In the

14

bath, in the bath! It's time to pull the plug out, time to mop the bath-room floor, The

Ped. * Ped. *

suddenly stronger

towel is in the cup-board, and the cup-board is next door! It's start-ed run-ning hot! Let's have a -

Da capo

- no-ther hour or more In the bath, _____ in the bath! 4.I can

CODA   *molto rit.*   *ff*   *falsetto*

end with-out the taps In the bath, _____ in the bath!

Ped.   *

15

Design for Living

When I started making money, when I started making friends,
We found a home as soon as we were able to.
We bought this little freehold for about a thousand more
Than the house our little house was once the stable to.
With charm, and colour values, wit, and structural alteration,
Now designed for graceful living, it has quite a reputation. . . .

We're terribly *House and Garden*
At Number Seven B,
We live in a most amusing mews—
Ever so very Contemporary!
We're terribly *House and Garden*;
The money that one spends
To make a place that won't disgrace
Our *House and Garden* friends!

We planned an uninhibited interior decor,
Curtains made of straw,
We've wall-papered the floor!
We don't know if we like it, but we're absolutely sure
There's no place like home sweet home.

We're fearfully *Maison Jardin*
At Number Seven B,
We've rediscovered the Chandelier—
Ever so very Contemporary!
We're terribly *House and Garden*.
Now at last we've got the chance,
The garden's full of furniture
And the house is full of plants!

Oh, it doesn't make for comfort
But it simply has to be;
You mustn't be left behind The Times
Furnishing Company!

Have you a home that cries out to your every visitor:
'Here lives somebody who is Exciting to Know!' No?

Why not . . .
Save little metal bottle-tops and nail them upside down to
the floor? This will give a sensation of walking on little
metal bottle-tops, turned upside down and nailed to the floor.

Why not . . .
get hold of an ordinary Northumbrian Spoke-shaver's Coracle,
paint it in contrasting stripes of Telephone Black and White,
and hang it up somewhere?

Why not . . .
keep, on some convenient shelving, a little cluster of clocks;
one for each member of the family, each an individual colour?
I like to keep mine twenty minutes fast, don't you?

Why not . . .
drop in one evening for a Mess of Pottage? *My* speciality.
Just aubergine and carnation petals—but with a six
shilling bottle of *Mule du Pape*, a feast fit for a king!
I'm delirious about our new cooker fitment with the
eye-level grill. This means that without my having
to bend down the hot fat can squirt straight into my eye!

We're frightfully *House and Garden*
At Number Seven B,
The walls are patterned with shrunken heads,
Ever so very Contemporary!
Our search for self-expression
Leaves us barely time for meals;
One day we're taking Liberty's in,
The next we're down at Heal's!

With wattle screens and little lamps and motifs here and there,
Mobiles in the air,
Ivy everywhere,
You mustn't be surprised to find a cactus in the chair,
But we call it home sweet home.

Oh, we're terribly *House and Garden*
As I think we said before,
But though Seven B is madly gay—
It wouldn't do for every day—
We actually *live* in Seven A,
In the house next door!

*"It's on the tip of my tongue . . . aren't you on the verge of becoming
a household name?"*

Main melody only (the introduction and the middle section were performed as spoken dialogue and extemporised recitative.)

18

-te – ri – or de – cor, ___ Cur-tains made of straw,_ We've wall-pa-pered the floor!_ We
mo – tifs here and there, ___ Mo – biles in the air, ___ I – vy ev – ery – where,_ You

don't know if we like it, but we're ab – so – lute – ly sure There's no place like home sweet
must-n't be sur-prised to find a cac – tus in the chair, But we call it home sweet

2nd time
omit 17 bars to ⊕

home.
home.   3. We're fear-ful-ly *Mai – son   Jar – din* ___ At Num – ber Se – ven

B,   We've re – dis – co – vered the Chan – de – lier— E – ver so ve – ry Con – tem – po – ra – ry! We're ter – ri – bly *House and*

19

Gar-den! Now at last we've got the chance, The gar-den's full of fur-ni-ture And the house is full of plants.

4.Oh, it does-n't make for com-fort But it sim-ply has to be;
7.Oh,we're ter-ri-bly *House and Gar-den* As I think I said be-fore, But though You

must-n't be left be-hind the times, You must-n't be left be-hind The Times Fur-nish-ing Com-pa-
Se-ven B is mad-ly gay— It would-n't do for

-ny! e-very day We actually live in Seven A, In the house next door.
(spoken)

in tempo

Ped.

20

Misalliance

The fragrant Honeysuckle spirals clockwise to the sun
And many other creepers do the same.
But some climb anti-clockwise; the Bindweed does, for one,
Or Convolvulus, to give her proper name.

Rooted on either side a door one of each species grew
And raced towards the window-ledge above;
Each corkscrewed to the lintel in the only way it knew,
Where they stopped, touched tendrils, smiled, and fell in love.

Said the right-handed Honeysuckle
To the left-handed Bindweed:
'Oh, let us get married
If our parents don't mind; we'd
Be loving and inseparable,
Inextricably entwined; we'd
Live happily ever after,'
Said the Honeysuckle to the Bindweed.

To the Honeysuckle's parents it came as a shock.
'The Bindweeds,' they cried, 'are inferior stock,
They're uncultivated, of breeding bereft;
We twine to the right—and they twine to the left!'

Said the anti-clockwise Bindweed
To the clockwise Honeysuckle:
'We'd better start saving,
Many a mickle makes a muckle,
Then run away for a honeymoon
And hope that our luck'll
Take a turn for the better,'
Said the Bindweed to the Honeysuckle.

A Bee who was passing remarked to them then:
'I've said it before, and I'll say it again;
Consider your off-shoots, if off-shoots there be,
They'll never receive any blessing from me!

'Poor little sucker, how will it learn
When it is climbing, which way to turn?
Right—left—what a disgrace!
Or it may go straight up and fall flat on its face!'

Said the right-hand thread Honeysuckle
To the left-hand thread Bind-
weed: 'It seems that against us
All fate has combined . . .
Oh my darling, oh my darling
Oh my darling Columbine,
Thou are lost and gone for ever,
We shall never intertwine.'

Together they found them the very next day.
They had pulled up their roots and just shrivelled away,
Deprived of that freedom for which we must fight—
To veer to the left or to veer to the right!

Gently ♩ = c.104

The fra-grant Ho-ney-su-ckle spi-rals clock-wise to the

sun And ma-ny o-ther cree-pers do the same. But some climb an-ti-clock-wise; the

Bind-weed does, for one, Or Con-vol-vu-lus, to give her pro-per name.

Root-ed on ei-ther side a door one of each spe-cies grew And raced to-wards the win-dow-ledge a -

- bove; Each cork-screwed to the lin-tel in the on - ly way it knew, Where they

stopped, touched ten-drils, smiled, and fell in love. Said the

right-han-ded Ho-ney-su-ckle To the left-han-ded Bind-weed:'Oh, let us get mar-ried If our pa-rents don't

mind; we'd Be lo-ving and in - se-pa-ra-ble In-ex-tri-ca-bly en - twined; we'd Live hap-pi-ly e-ver

24

af-ter,' Said the Ho-ney-su-ckle to the Bind-weed.

To the

Ho-ney-su-ckle's pa-rents it came as a shock. 'The Bind-weeds,' they cried,'Are in - fe - ri - or

stock, They're un-cul-ti - va-ted, of breed-ing be - reft; We twine to the right—and they twine to the

left!' Said the an-ti-clock-wise Bind-weed To the clock-wise Ho-ney - su-ckle: 'We'd bet-ter start

sa - ving, Ma-ny a mi-ckle makes a mu-ckle, Then run a-way for a Ho-ney-moon And hope that our

luck'll Take a turn for the bet-ter,' Said the Bind-weed to the Ho-ney-su-ckle.

A Bee who was pas-sing re-marked to them then: 'I've said it be -

più forte

- fore, and I'll say it a - gain; Con - si-der your off-shoots, if off-shoots there be, They'll

più forte

26

Strict waltz ♪ = 152

ne-ver re – ceive a – ny bles-sing from me!' 'Poor lit-tle su-cker, how will it learn

When it is climb-ing, which way to turn? Right — left — what a dis-grace! Or it

poco rit. Back to

may go straight up and fall flat on its face!' Said the

slower tempo (♪ = 132)

right-hand thread Ho-ney-su-ckle To the left-hand thread Bind-weed:'It seems that a - gainst us All

27

fate has com - bined... Oh my dar-ling, oh my dar-ling, Oh my dar - ling Co - lum - bine, Thou art

lost and gone for - e - ver, We shall ne - ver in - ter - twine.' To - ge - ther they

found them the ve - ry next day. They had pulled up their roots and just shri - velled a - way, De -

-prived of that free - dom for which we must fight— To veer to the left or to veer to the right!

28

The Gasman Cometh

'Twas on a MONDAY morning
The GASMAN came to call;
The gas tap wouldn't turn—I wasn't getting gas at all.
He tore out all the skirting boards
To try and find the main,
And I had to call a CARPENTER to put them back again.
    Oh, it all makes work for the working man to do!

'Twas on a TUESDAY morning
The CARPENTER came round;
He hammered and he chiselled and he said: 'Look what I've found!
Your joists are full of dry-rot
But I'll put it all to rights.'
Then he nailed right through a cable and out went all the lights.
    Oh, it all makes work for the working man to do!

'Twas on a WEDNESDAY morning
The ELECTRICIAN came;
He called me 'Mr Sanderson' (which isn't quite my name).
He couldn't reach the fuse box
Without standing on the bin
And his foot went through a window—so I called a GLAZIER in.
    Oh, it all makes work for the working man to do!

'Twas on a THURSDAY morning
The GLAZIER came along,
With his blow-torch and his putty and his merry Glazier's song;
He put another pane in—
It took no time at all—
But I had to get a PAINTER in to come and paint the wall.
    Oh, it all makes work for the working man to do!

'Twas on a FRIDAY morning
The PAINTER made a start;
With undercoats and overcoats he painted every part,
Every nook and every cranny,
But I found when he was gone
He'd painted over the gas tap and I couldn't turn it on!
    Oh, it all makes work for the working man to do!

On SATURDAY and SUNDAY they do no work at all:
So 'twas on a MONDAY morning that the GASMAN came to call!

"A real gas repair man would have brought the wrong fittings."

Brightly ♩. = 120

1.'Twas on a MON – DAY morn - ing The GAS – MAN came to call; The gas tap would-n't turn— I was-n't get-ting gas at all. ___ He tore out all the skirt - ing boards To try and find the

30

main, And I had to call a CAR - PEN-TER to put them back a - gain, Oh, it

1. *All but last verse*

all makes work for the work - ing man to do! ___

2. *Last time*

verses 2 - 5 'Twas do! On SA-TUR-DAY ___ and SUN-DAY ___ They do no work at

A tempo

all, So 'twas on a MON - DAY morn - ing that the GAS - MAN came to call!

Song of the Weather

JANUARY brings the snow,
Makes your feet and fingers glow.

FEBRUARY's ice and sleet
Freeze the toes right off your feet.

Welcome MARCH with wintry wind—
Would thou wert not so unkind!

APRIL brings the sweet spring showers,
On and on for hours and hours.

Farmers fear unkindly MAY—
Frost by night and hail by day.

JUNE just rains and never stops—
Thirty days and spoils the crops.

In JULY the sun is hot.
Is it shining? No, it's not.

AUGUST, cold and dank and wet,
Brings more rain than any yet.

Bleak SEPTEMBER's mist and mud
Is enough to chill the blood.

Then OCTOBER adds a gale,
Wind and slush and rain and hail.

Dark NOVEMBER brings the fog—
Should not do it to a dog.

Freezing wet DECEMBER, then
Bloody JANUARY again!

JANUARY brings the snow . . .

Pillar to Post

The Traffic Signs are gleaming—
  They reflect a cheerful light;
The Standard Lamps are beaming—
  They get lit up every night;
The Fire Alarm is thinking
  Of some funny false alarms;
The Police Call-Box is winking
  With a Sergeant in her arms.

Oh, all the street seems happy,
  But there's one who's standing by,
A lonely little fellow
  Who is trying not to cry;
While all the rest are happy
  His courageous heart is not,
And I hear him sadly singing
  As a tear runs down his slot:

'Pity the poor little Pillar-Box
  Standing in the rain all day,
Tired and weary, weak and shivery,
  Waiting for the next delivery.
Nobody cares for the Pillar-Box
  Or asks him out to play,
So pity the pretty little Pillar-Box
  Standing in the rain all day.'

Listen when you post a letter
  And you'll hear a muffled sob,
For he longs for something better
  Than a letter down his gob.
It's cruel to dishearten
  Little Pillar-Boxes so,
But no one tries to start an
  R.S.P.C. G.P.O.!

A solitary figure
  In a little coat of red,
He always does his duty,
  Holding high his weary head.
He never tries to run away
  Or bite the Postman's hand
And so I feed him sandwiches
  To show I understand.

Pity the poor little Pillar-Box
  Standing in the rain all day.
Gazing out in each direction
  Hoping for the next collection.
Everyone owes to the Pillar-Box
  A debt they can't repay,
So pity the pretty little Pillar-Box . . .
  Pillar-Box, you're O.K.!
  Standing in the rain all day.

Gently aloof: rubato ♩ = 112

mp

1. The Traf-fic Signs are gleam-ing—They re-
4. Lis-ten when you post a let-ter And you'll

-flect a cheer-ful light; The Stand-ard lamps are beam-ing—They get lit up e-ver-y night; The
hear a muf-fled sob, For he longs for some-thing bet-ter Than a let-ter down his gob. It's

Fire A-larm is think-ing Of some fun-ny false a-larms; The Po-lice Call-Box is wink-ing With a
cru-el to dis-heart-en Lit-tle Pil-lar Box-es so, But no one tries to start an R. S.

poco f   *mf broadly*

Ser-geant in her arms. 2.Oh, all the street is hap-py, But there's one who's stand-ing by, A
P. C. G. P. O! 5.A so-li-ta-ry fi-gure In a lit-tle coat of red, He

poco f   *mf*

lone-ly lit-tle fel-low who is try-ing not to cry; While all the rest are hap-py His cou-
al-ways does his du-ty, Hold-ing high his wea-ry head. He ne-ver tries to run a-way Or

rit.

- ra-geous heart is not, And I hear him sad-ly sing-ing As a tear runs down his slot:
bite the Post-man's hand And so I feed him sand-wi-ches To show I un-der-stand.

A bit livelier, and in stricter tempo

3.
6. Pi-ty the poor lit-tle Pil-lar-Box Stand-ing in the rain all day.

Tired and wea-ry, weak and shi-ve-ry, Wai-ting for the next de-li-ve-ry.
Gaz-ing out in each di-rec-tion Ho-ping for the next col-lec-tion.

No - bo - dy cares for the Pil-lar-Box Or asks him out to play, So
Ev - ery-one owes to the Pil-lar-Box A debt they can't re - pay, So

pi - ty the pret-ty lit-tle Pil-lar-Box
(2nd. time) Lit-tle

Stand-ing in the rain all

Tempo I **molto allargando** *cresc.* *f*

day. Pil-lar-Box, you're O. K.! _____ Stand-ing in the

Tempo I *mp* **poco rit.** **a tempo**

rain _____ all day.

mp

Rain on the Plage

When it's raining on the Plage
There is water everywhere.
Can this be the Riviera?
It's more like a Rivière!
What we spend on hot potage
We shall save on Ambre Solaire,
But it might have been plus sage
To have found some other Plage
Such as Bournemouth or Swanage
Back in sunny Angleterre.

When it's raining on the Plage
There is nowhere else to go;
All the cinemas are showing
'Passeport à Pimlico'.
They've collected our bagages
And we're waiting for the train.
When they wish us Bon Voyage
We shall murmur, 'Quel dommage:
Une si jolie petite Plage
If it wasn't for the rain.'

Gracefully ♩. = 60   poco rit.   a tempo

1.When it's rain - ing on the Pla - ge _____
(2.)   rain - ing on the Pla - ge _____

_____ There is wa - ter ev - ery - where. Can this be the Ri - vi -
_____ There is no - where else to go; All the ci - ne - mas are

- e - ra? _____ It's more like a Ri - vi - ère! _____ What we spend on
show-ing _____ 'Pas - se - port à Pim - li - co'. _____ They've col - lec - ted

hot po - ta - ge _____ We shall save on Ambre So - laire, _____ But it
our ba - ga - ges _____ And we're wait - ing for the train. _____ When they

39

might have been plus sa-ge _____ To have found some o - ther Pla-ge _____
wish us Bon Voy - a - ge _____ We shall mur - mur, 'Quel dom - ma - ge: _____

_____ Such as Bourne-mouth or Swa - na-ge _____ Back in sun - ny An - gle -
_____ Une si jo - lie pe - tite Pla-ge _____ If it was - n't for the

-terre _____ 2.When it's _____ the

rain, _____ the rain, the rain.'

Ped.

Motor Perpetuo

In the course of an average lifetime
It has been said
A man spends twenty precious years
Asleep in bed;
Seven more in eating
Or drinking at the bar
And most of the remainder
Trying to park his car . . .

Parking the car, parking the car,
Yellow bands, unloading bays,
Other side Uneven Days,
Up and down the backstreets,
You don't know where you are;
You feel like Noah in the Ark
Afloat in what is now Iraq
When he found no place to disembark in,
Parking the car!

There's a place . . . Where? Look, back in there!
No, it's the wrong side of the zebra crossing.
No, it isn't.
Then it must be less than 25 feet from a hump-backed bridge.
It's a perfectly good, empty parking space.
What, in this street, at this time in the morning?
Drive on—it's a trap!

Mustn't stop and mustn't wait,
Mustn't even hesitate . . .
'Nothing could be sweeter
Than to find an empty meter
In the morning'.

For the Trooping of the Colour
They come from near and far
But all they ever see of it
Is the parking of the car.

"Why the devil can't you pick a space your own size?"

Parking the car, parking the car,
Yellow bands, unloading bays,
Other side Uneven Days.
Hear the driver's mournful shout:
'Are you going in or coming out?'
Every time we feel we must stop
It's a crossing or a bus stop;
Every garage where we pull up
Has a notice, 'Sorry, full up'.

Parking the car, parking the car,
Several thousand miles a year,
Most of them in bottom gear,
Crawling down the main street
Without a guiding star—
Towards the closing of the day
We turn and head the other way.
We know we won't be home until it's dark,
And we'll never ever find a place to park!

(Main melody for second and final stanzas only)

42

don't know where you are; You feel like No - ah in the Ark. A -
- out a guid - ing star — To - wards the clos - ing of the day We

1.
float in what is now I - raq When he found no place to dis - em - bark in,
turn and head the o - ther way. We

2. **a tempo**
Park-ing the car. know we won't be home un - til it's dark, _____

— And we'll ne - ver e - ver find a place to park. _____

43

The Slow Train

Miller's Dale for Tideswell . . .
Kirby Muxloe . . .
Mow Cop and Scholar Green . . .

No more will I go to Blandford Forum and Mortehoe
On the slow train from Midsomer Norton and Mumby Road.
No churns, no porter, no cat on a seat
At Chorlton-cum-Hardy or Chester-le-Street.
We won't be meeting again
On the Slow Train.

I'll travel no more from Littleton Badsey to Openshaw.
At Long Stanton I'll stand well clear of the doors no more.
No whitewashed pebbles, no Up and no Down
From Formby Four Crosses to Dunstable Town.
I won't be going again
On the Slow Train.

On the Main Line and the Goods Siding
The grass grows high
At Dog Dyke, Tumby Woodside
And Trouble House Halt.

The Sleepers sleep at Audlem and Ambergate.
No passenger waits on Chittening platform or Cheslyn Hay.
No one departs, no one arrives
From Selby to Goole, from St Erth to St Ives.
They've all passed out of our lives
On the Slow Train, on the Slow Train.

Cockermouth for Buttermere . . . on the Slow Train,
Armley Moor Arram . . .
Pye Hill and Somercotes . . .
Windmill End . . . on the Slow Train.

Gently ♩.=46

(spoken) Miller's Dale for Tides-well... Kirkby Mux-loe... Mow Cop and Scholar Green.. No more will I go to Bland-ford Fo-rum and Mor-te-hoe _____ On the slow train from Mid-so-mer Nor-ton and Mum — by Road. No churns, no por-ter, no

senza **Ped.**

p

sim.

45

cat on a seat At Chorl-ton-cum-Har-dy or Ches-ter-le-Street. We

won't be meet-ing a - gain On the Slow Train. I'll

8va con **Ped**.

tra-vel no more from Lit-tle-ton Bad-sey to Op - en-shaw. At

Long Stan-ton I'll stand well clear of the doors no more. No

46

white-washed peb-bles, no Up and no Down From Form — by Four Cros-ses to

Dun — sta — ble Town. I won't be go-ing a — gain On the

poco più mosso

Slow Train. On the Main Line and the Goods Si — ding

con **Ped**.

The grass grows high At Dog Dyke, Tum — by Wood — side And

rit.

Trou-ble House Halt. The Sleep-ers sleep _____ at Aud-lem and

pp *colla voce*

tempo primo

Am - ber-gate. No pas-sen-ger waits on Chit-ten-ing plat-form or

con **Ped**.

Ches - lyn Hay. No one de-parts, no one ar-rives From

sim.

Sel - by to Goole from St Erth to St Ives. They've all passed out of our

48

lives _____ On the Slow Train, on the Slow Train, _____

sim.

(spoken) Cockermouth for Buttermere...   on the   Slow   Train,

pp

pp

(spoken) Armley Moor Arram.....Pye Hill and Somercotes...   on the   Slow   Train.

(spoken) Windmill End.

poco rit.

Last of the Line

When the streets are silent have you wondered at the sight
Of a little group outside the Terminus?
By the dark deserted London Transport Depot every night?
Don't wonder any longer—'cause it's us!

Three broken-hearted tram-drivers with nothing else to do
But lift our weary heads to heaven above,
And sing for all to hear as we wipe away a tear
With the corner of an old tram-driver's glove—

    Good-bye old Tram!
    No matter where I am
    I'll think of you until my memory fails.
    We'd drive through fog or shower
    At fifteen miles per hour
    And yet you'd always keep us on the rails.

    Now worn and scarred
    Towards the Breaker's Yard
    You have journeyed where they issue no returns.
    Old pal of mine,
    They've started digging up the line:
    Good-bye old Tram!

Diving down the Kingsway Tunnel like the gaping jaws of hell
To the river, where you'd give her all you'd got!
Oh, the sight of sparks a-flying! Oh, the jangling of the bell!
Oh, the scent of wooden brake-blocks running hot!

From Woolwich Park to Camberwell, from Highgate Hill to Bow,
On to Wapping, only stopping by request,
Down a hill or round a bend we would drive at either end
And we never knew which end we loved the best!

    Good-bye old Tram!
    In every traffic jam
    You'd patiently endure your heavy load.
    Where'er the tram wires led,
    Drawing power from overhead,
    You took us down the middle of life's road!

L.P.T.B.
Has signed your R.I.P.,
And here we mourn your passing down the line,
Until some day
We drive you through the Milky Way:
Good-bye old Tram!
They won't get us
To drive their ruddy trolley-bus!
Good-bye old Tram!

51

De - pot ev - ery night? Don't won - der an - y lon - ger- 'cause it's us,   oh yes, it's us!   2. Three
jang-ling of the bell! Oh, the scent of wood-en brake-blocks run-ning hot,   yes run-ning hot!   6. From

bro - ken-heart-ed tram-dri-vers with no-thing else to do   But lift our wea-ry heads to heaven a -
Wool-wich Park to Cam-ber-well, from High-gate Hill to Bow,   On to Wap-ping on - ly stop-ping by re-

-bove,   And sing for all to hear   as we   wipe a - way a tear With the
-quest,   Down a   hill or round a bend   we would   drive at ei-ther end And we

Ped.   *

rit.   a tempo

cor-ner of an old tram-dri-ver's glove, tram dri-ver's glove— 3. Good - bye, old Tram! No
ne-ver knew which end we loved the best, we loved the best! 7. Good - bye, old Tram! In

52

mat-ter where I am   I'll think of you un – til my me – mory fails, me-mory fails. We'd
ev – ery traffic jam   You'd pa – tient-ly en – dure your hea – vy load, hea-vy load. Wher-

drive thro' fog or show-er   At fif-teen miles per hour   And yet you'd al-ways keep us on the
e'er the tram wires led, _ Draw-ing power from o – ver-head,   You took us down the mid-dle of life's

rails, on the rails. 4.Now worn and scarred   To – wards the Break-er's Yard   You have
road, of life's road! 8.L. P. T. B.   Has signed your R. I. P.,   And

jour-neyed where they is – sue no re – turns.   Old pal of mine, They've
here we mourn your pas-sing down the line,   Un – til some day We

53

start-ed dig-ging up the line: Good - bye old ——— Tram!
drive you thro' the Mil - ky Way: Good - bye old ——— Tram!

5.Div-ing They

won't get us To drive their rud-dy trol-ley-bus! Good - bye old Tram!

Ped. ✻ Ped. ✻

54

A Transport of Delight (The Omnibus)

Some talk of a Lagonda,
Some like a smart M.G.,
Or for Bonnie Army Lorry
They'd lay them doon and dee.
Such means of locomotion
Seem rather dull to us—
The Driver and Conductor
Of a London Omnibus.

Hold very tight please, ting-ting!

When you are lost in London
And you don't know where you are,
You'll hear my voice a-calling:
'Pass further down the car!'
And very soon you'll find yourself
Inside the Terminus
    In a London Transport
    Diesel-engined
    Ninety-seven horse-power
    Omnibus!

Along the Queen's great highway
I drive my merry load
At twenty miles per hour
In the middle of the road;
We like to drive in convoys—
We're most gregarious;
    The big six-wheeler
    Scarlet-painted
    London Transport
    Diesel-engined
    Ninety-seven horse-power
    Omnibus!

Earth has not anything to show more fair!
Mind the stairs! Mind the stairs!
Earth has not anything to show more fair!
Any more fares? Any more fares?

When cabbies try to pass me,
Before they overtakes,
I sticks me flippin' hand out
As I jams on all me brakes!
Them jackal taxi-drivers
Can only swear and cuss,
 Behind that monarch of the road,
 Observer of the Highway Code,
 That big six-wheeler
 Scarlet-painted
 London Transport
 Diesel-engined
 Ninety-seven horse-power
 Omnibus!

I stops when I'm requested
Although it spoils the ride,
So he can shout: 'Get aht of it!
We're full right up inside!'

We don't ask much for wages,
We only want fair shares,
So cut down all the stages,
And stick up all the fares.
If tickets cost a pound apiece
Why should you make a fuss?
It's worth it just to ride inside
That thirty-foot-long by ten-foot-wide,
 Inside that monarch of the road,
 Observer of the Highway Code,
 That big six-wheeler
 Scarlet-painted
 London Transport
 Diesel-engined
 Ninety-seven horse-power
 Omnibus!

Poco moderato
(rather freely)

2 voices

1.Some talk of a La - gon - da, Some like a smart M.

G., Or for Bon-nie Ar-my Lor-ry They'd lay them doon and dee. Such means of lo-co-

DRIVER CONDUCTOR BOTH **Allegretto** ♩=120

-mo-tion Seem ra-ther dull to us— The Dri-ver and Con-duc-tor Of a Lon-don Om-ni-

CONDUCTOR

- bus. Hold ve-ry tight please,_ ting-ting! Hold ve-ry tight please,_ ting-ting! 2.When

you are lost in Lon-don And you don't know where you are, You'll hear my voice a-
(3.)-long the Queen's great High-way I drive my mer-ry load At twen-ty miles per

-cal-ling: 'Pass fur-ther down the car!' And ve-ry soon you'll find your-self In - side the Ter-mi -
hour In the middle of the road; We like to drive in con-voys— We're most gre-ga - ri -

BOTH

1

- nus In a Lon-don Trans-port Die-sel-en-gined Ninety-seven horse-power Om-ni-bus!
- ous; The big six-wheel-er Scarlet-painted

DRIVER **2**

3.A - Lon-don Trans-port Die-sel-en-gined Ninety-seven horse-power Om-ni-bus!

CONDUCTOR

Earth has not a - ny-thing to show more fair! Mind the stairs! _____ Mind the

Ped. ❋ Ped. Ped.

58

stairs! _____ Earth has not a-ny-thing to show more fair! A-ny more fares? _____

A-ny more fares? _____ 4. When cab-bies try to pass me, Be - fore they o-ver-

-takes, I sticks me flip-pin' hand out As I jams on all me brakes! Them jackal ta-xi-

- dri-vers Can on-ly swear and cuss, Be -hind that mo-narch of the road, Ob - ser-ver of the

59

CONDUCTOR   DRIVER   CONDUCTOR   DRIVER   BOTH

Highway Code, That big six-wheeler Scarlet-painted London Transport Diesel-engined Ninety-seven horse-power

Om-ni-bus!

DRIVER

I stops when I'm re-quest-ed Al-though it spoils the ride, So

CONDUCTOR

he can shout (spoken) 'Get aht of it! We're full right up inside!'

BOTH

We don't ask much for

wa-ges, We on-ly want fair shares, So cut down all the sta-ges, And stick up all the fares. If

60

ti-ckets cost a pound a – piece Why should you make a fuss? It's worth it just to ride in-side That

CONDUCTOR   DRIVER

CONDUCTOR   DRIVER

thir-ty-foot-long by ten-foot-wide, In – side that mo-narch of the road, Ob – ser-ver of the

BOTH

High-way Code, That big six-wheel-er Scar-let – paint-ed Lon – don Trans-port Die -. sel – en – gined

CONDUCTOR

Ninety-seven horse-power   Ninety-seven horse-power Om-ni-bus! Hold very tight
                                                                                    please!
                                                                           (spoken)

ff   sf sf

61

Twenty Tons of TNT

I have seen it estimated:
    Somewhere between death and birth
There are now three thousand million
    People living on this earth
And the stock-piled mass destruction
Of the Nuclear Powers-That-Be
Equals—for each man or woman—
    Twenty tons of TNT.

Every man of every nation
    (Twenty tons of TNT)
Shall receive this allocation
    Twenty tons of TNT.
Texan, Bantu, Slav or Maori,
Argentine or Singhalee,
Every maiden brings this dowry
    Twenty tons of TNT.

Not for thirty silver shilling
    Twenty tons of TNT.
Twenty thousand pounds a killing—
    Twenty tons of TNT.
Twenty hundred years of teaching,
Give to each his legacy,
Plato, Buddha, Christ or Lenin,
    Twenty tons of TNT.

Father, Mother, Son and Daughter,
    Twenty tons of TNT.
Give us land and seed and water,
    Twenty tons of TNT.
Children have no need of sharing;
At each new nativity
Come the ghostly Magi bearing
    Twenty tons of TNT.

Ends the tale that has no sequel
    Twenty tons of TNT.
Now in death are all men equal
    Twenty tons of TNT.
Teach me how to love my neighbour,
Do to him as he to me;
Share the fruits of all our labour
    Twenty tons of TNT.

Stern and forceful ♩ = 80

(verse 1) I have seen it e-sti-ma-ted: Some-where be-tween
(all other verses) E - very man of e-very na-tion (Twen - ty tons of

death and birth There are now three thou-sand mil-lion Peo-ple li-ving on this earth
T. N. T.) Shall re-ceive this al-lo-ca-tion: Twen - ty tons of T. N. T.

And the stock-piled mass des-truc-tion Of the Nu - clear Powers-That-Be E - quals for each
Tex - an, Ban-tu, Slav or Mao-ri, Ar - gen-tine or Sin - gha-lee, E - very mai - den

poco rit.   **1.** *All but last verse*   **2.** *Last time*
              a tempo   *a tempo*   *mp a tempo*   *poco rit.*

man or wo - man   Twen-ty tons of T. N. T.   *(knock)*   Twen-ty tons of T. N. T.
brings this dow - ry:

✴ *(Optional before 2nd.and 3rd.verses: knock instead of piano chords.*
  N.B. 3rd.verse may be sung unaccompanied.)

The Reluctant Cannibal

Seated one day at the Tom-tom I heard a welcome shout from the kitchen: 'Come and get it! Roast leg of insurance salesman!' (Um, um . . .) A chorus of yums ran round the table (Yum yum yum yum yum . . .), except for Junior, who pushed away his shell, got up from his log and said:

I don't want any part of it!	*What? Why not?*
I don't eat people,	*Uh?*
I won't eat people,	*Ummmmm?*
I don't eat people,	*I must be going deaf!*
Eating people is wrong!	*It's wrong?*
Don't eat people,	*Are you out of your mind?*
Won't eat people,	*What's the matter with the lad?*
Don't eat people,	*He keeps on repeating . . .*
Eating people is bad!	
	But people have always eaten people!
	What else is there to eat?
	If the Ju-Ju had meant us not to eat people,
	He wouldn't have made us of meat!
Don't eat people,	*Oh, no!*
Won't eat people,	*All the day long . . .*
Don't eat people,	*He keeps on repeating . . .*
Eating people's bad!	

Well I never heard a more ridiculous idea in all my born days. I suppose you realise, son, that if this was to get around, we might never get self-government?

I won't eat people.

Have you been talking with one of your mothers again? You're not getting to be one of those cranks who think that eating people is cruel, are you? Seeing a man sitting in a pot and you think he's suffering? Oh, it's not like that at all. Why, he's sitting there in the nice warm water with all the carrots and noodles and things thinking of all the pleasure and happiness he's going to give to all the rest of us. That man in the pot there really enjoys it!

Eating people is wrong!

Look son, I admire your sincerity. Always be sincere, whether you mean it or not. But you're young. How wonderful to be young! When you're young you think that you can change the whole world overnight, even eating people. I know. I've been young myself. But take it from your old dad: as you grow older you've just got to learn to take the world as it is!

I won't let another man pass my lips!

I know why you say, 'Don't eat people'. Because you're a coward, a yellow-livered coward: that's your trouble, Francis. You wouldn't mind eating people if you weren't afraid of ending up in the pot yourself. Go on like this and you're liable to get me into hot water!

I won't eat people,
I don't eat people,
Eating people is wrong!

Communist!

Going around saying, 'Don't eat people',
Is the way to make people hate yer.
Always have eaten people,
Always will eat people.
You can't change human nature!

I won't eat people,
I don't eat people,
Won't eat people,
Don't eat people,
I won't eat people,
I don't eat people,
Eating people is out!

Look, will you listen to your old dad?

It must have been someone he ate . . .

See here, son . . .

I give up. And he used to be a regular Anthropophaguy. If this crazy idealist notion should catch on, it might ruin our entire internal economy. Fortunately that isn't very likely. Why, you might as well say, 'Don't fight people!'

Don't fight people?
Don't fight . . .?
Ridiculous!

That's what I said. Don't fight people.
Yeah . . . don't . . .
That's my boy!

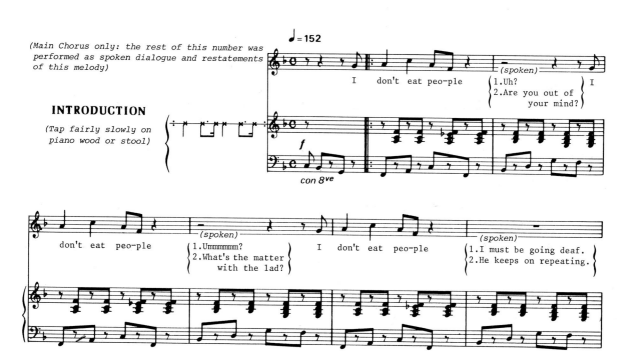

(Main Chorus only: the rest of this number was performed as spoken dialogue and restatements of this melody)

INTRODUCTION

(Tap fairly slowly on piano wood or stool)

I don't eat peo-ple

(spoken)
1. Uh?
2. Are you out of your mind?

I

don't eat peo-ple

(spoken)
1. Ummmmmm?
2. What's the matter with the lad?

I don't eat peo-ple

(spoken)
1. I must be going deaf.
2. He keeps on repeating.

65

P * * P * B * * * * B * * D * * * * * *

Ma's out, Pa's out—let's talk rude:
    Pee – Po – Belly – Bum – Drawers!
Dance in the garden in the nude:
    Pee – Po – Belly – Bum – Drawers!
Let's write rude words all down our street,
Stick out our tongues at the people we meet,
Let's have an intellectual treat:
    Pee – Po – Belly – Bum – Drawers!

What kind of talk is the Dons' delight?
    Pee – Po – Belly – Bum – Drawers.
What's on every newstand in sight?
    Playboy – Belly – Bum – Drawers.
What TV comedy's loved the best?
What did Illingworth say at the Final Test?
What is Prince Philip's favourite jest?
    Pee – Po – Belly – Bum – Drawers.

Danny La Rue's in a double bill:
    Pee – Po – Belly – Bum – Drawers.
Christopher Robin meets *Fanny Hill*:
    Pooh Bear – Belly – Bum – Drawers!
Kenneth Tynan has given his all
And in *Oh Calcutta* they have a ball . . .
'Cause the higher the brow the harder they fall:
    Pee – Po – Belly – Bum – Drawers.

Ken Russell's filming in Regent's Park
    Pee – Po – Belly – Bum – Drawers,
Full Frontal Composers, Bach to Bach
    Pee – Po – Belly – Bum – Drawers,
From the folk-song scene to the world of Pop
They get their words from the Porno Shop—
Things seem to start where they used to stop
    With Pee – Po – Belly – Bum – Drawers!

Brightly ♩ = 72

1. Ma's out Pa's out let's talk rude: Pee-Po-Bel-ly-Bum—Drawers! Dance in the gar - den

in the nude: Pee - Po - Bel-ly-Bum — Drawers! Let's write rude words all down our street,

Stick out our tongues at the peo-ple we meet Let's have an in - tel — lec - tual treat:

1. All but last verse

Pee - Po - Bel-ly-Bum Drawers! used to stop With Pee - Po - Bel-ly-Bel-ly-Bum - Bum —

2. Last time only

68

-Pee – Po – Bel-ly-Bum – Pee – Po – Bel-ly-Bum – Pee – Po – Bel-ly – Bum – Drawers!

Budget Song

There's a hole in my Budget, dear Callaghan, dear Callaghan,
There's a hole in my Budget, dear P.M. my dear.

Then mend it dear Healey, dear Healey, dear Healey,
Then mend it dear Healey, dear Healey my dear.

But how shall I mend it, dear Callaghan, dear Callaghan?
But how shall I mend it, dear P.M. my dear?

By building up exports, dear Healey, dear Healey,
By increased production, dear Healey my dear.

But that means working harder, dear Callaghan, dear Callaghan,
And the workers must have more incentives, my dear.

Then decrease taxation, dear Healey, dear Healey,
And raise all their wages, dear Healey my dear.

70

And where is the money to come from, dear Callaghan?
But where is the money to come from, my dear?

Why out of your Budget, dear Healey, dear Healey,
Out of your Budget, dear Healey my dear.

But there's a hole in my Budget, dear Callaghan, dear Callaghan,
There's a hole in my Budget, dear P.M. my dear.

Then mend it dear Healey, dear Healey, dear Healey,
Then mend it dear Healey, dear Healey my dear.

But how shall . . .

*This song is a dialogue between the Prime Minister and Chancellor of the day.
The two performers wander round the stage or room in a slow inflationary spiral.*

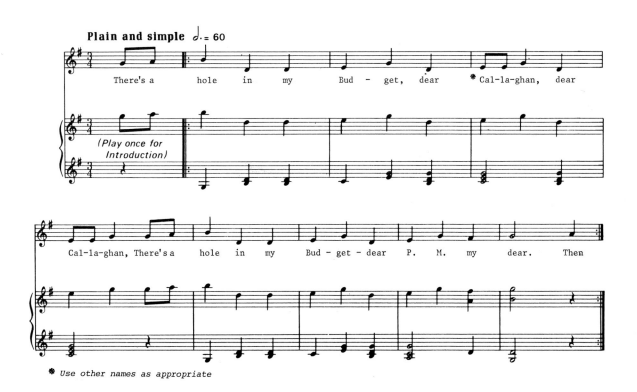

Plain and simple ♩. = 60

There's a hole in my Bud - get, dear *Cal-la-ghan, dear

(Play once for Introduction)

Cal-la-ghan, There's a hole in my Bud - get - dear P. M. my dear. Then

* Use other names as appropriate

THE CAR COST THREE THOUSAND POUNDS — TO SAY NOTHING OF ITS UPKEEP — AND HER COAT SEVEN HUNDRED AND FIFTY GUINEAS.   YET SHE EMPLOYS THEM TO MOTOR SOME FORTY ODD MILES —

INTO TOWN IN ORDER TO TAKE PART IN A STRUGGLE TO SECURE THE ADVANTAGE OF A SPECIAL REDUCTION OF THREE HALFPENCE PER YARD ON SOME CRETONNE SHE NEEDS.

Ballad for the Rich

We're the *Noblesse* of Burke's Peerage,
Now *Obleeged* to travel steerage
In the Ship of State
With fellow travellers we hate . . .

The *Daily Herald* hates us,
The *Worker* execrates us;
They wouldn't take us in if we were dying in a ditch!
A last resort we dare not try
With duty on our death so high—
Oh, no-one wants the poor, deserving rich!

It's the same the whole world over—
It's the Rich who get the blame;
It's the Poor who get the pleasure;
Is it not a crying shame?

While we rich must queue for taxis
How the poor man sneers at us,
Riding on a workman's ticket
In his special worker's bus!

When his five-day week is ended
Then the poor man can relax,
But on Saturdays and Sundays
We must work to earn our tax!

It's the same the whole world over—
It's the Rich who get the blame;
It's the Poor who get the pleasure;
Is it not a crying shame?

While we rich will always tell you
That we can't afford one yet,
All the poor without exception
Have a television set!

See my eldest, down from Oxford,
Seeking work from yard to yard,
But the idle workers spurn him—
Born without a Union Card!

It's the same the whole world over—
It's the Rich who get the blame;
It's the Poor who get the pleasure;
Is it not a crying shame?

In the gilded picture-palace
Sits the poor man at his ease,
While we rich in squalid night-clubs
Cringe in fear of the Police!

We congratulate the Poor
Now they're socially secure—
But there are other classes
Besides the Masses!

It is the same the whole world over—
It is the well-to-do who incur all the odium
While the indigent reap all the benefits.
Don't you consider that this is an intolerable discrimination?

The first two verses and the last verse but one should be declaimed or, if possible, sung recitative to an extemporised accompaniment; the words of the last verse should be fitted in over the main Chorus tune.

74

All Gall

Frère Jacques
I'm all right
Son et lumière
VIVE DE GAULLE

This old man he played ONE,
He played knick-knack at Verdun.
Cognac, Armagnac, Burgundy and Beaune,
This old man came rolling home.

This old man—World War TWO—
He told Churchill what to do.
Free French General—Crosses of Lorraine;
He came rolling home again.

This old man he played TROIS,
'Vive la France! La France c'est moi!
Gimcrack governments—call me if you please:
Colombey-les-deux-Eglises.'

This old man he played FOUR;
Choose de Gaulle or Civil War!
Come back President, govern by decree.
Referendum: Oui – oui – oui!

75

This old man he played FIVE,
'France is safe, I'm still alive.'
Plastiques, Pompidou, sing the Marseillaise:
ALGÉRIE N'EST PAS FRANÇAISE.

This old man he played SIX:
'France and England they don't mix.
Eytie, Benelux, Germany and me—
That's my market recipe!'

This old man, SEVEN and EIGHT,
You can count me out of NAT-
O. Farewell Pentagon, find another land.
Goodbye Macnamara's Band!

This old man he played NINE,
'Ban the Bomb (except for mine!)'
Bonjour Moscow, Leningrad and all,
This old man looks eight foot tall.

This old man he played TEN,
He'll play Nick till God knows when.
Cognac, Armagnac, Burgundy and Beaune,
This old man thinks he's Saint Joan!

♩ = 132

Frè - re Jac - ques Frè - re Jac - ques I'm all right I'm all right

Son et lu-mi-è - re Son et lu-mi-è - re *(shouted)* VIVE DE GAULLE!

♩ = 80

1.This old man he played ONE, He played knick-knack at Ver-dun.

Co - gnac, Ar-ma-gnac, Bur-gun-dy and Beaune, This old man came rol - ling home.

Song of Patriotic Prejudice

The rottenest bits of these islands of ours
We've left in the hands of three unfriendly powers;
Examine the Irishman, Welshman or Scot,
You'll find he's a stinker as likely as not!
   The English, the English, the English are best!
   I wouldn't give tuppence for all of the rest!

The Scotsman is mean, as we're all well aware,
And bony and blotchy and covered with hair;
He eats salty porridge, he works all the day
And he hasn't got Bishops to show him the way.
   The English, the English, the English are best!
   I wouldn't give tuppence for all of the rest!

The Irishman now our contempt is beneath;
He sleeps in his boots, and he lies in his teeth;
He blows up policemen, or so I have heard,
And blames it on Cromwell and William the Third.
   The English are noble, the English are nice,
   And worth any other at double the price!

The Welshman's dishonest—he cheats when he can—
And little and dark, more like monkey than man;
He works underground with a lamp in his hat
And sings far too loud, far too often, and flat.
   The English, the English, the English are best!
   I wouldn't give tuppence for all of the rest!

And crossing the Channel one cannot say much
For the French or the Spanish, the Danish or Dutch;
The Germans are German, the Russians are Red
And the Greeks and Italians eat garlic in bed.
   The English are moral, the English are good
   And clever and modest and misunderstood.

And all the world over each nation's the same—
They've simply no notion of Playing the Game;
They argue with Umpires, they cheer when they've won,
And they practice beforehand, which spoils all the fun!
   The English, the English, the English are best!
   So up with the English and down with the rest!

It's not that they're wicked or naturally bad:
It's knowing they're *foreign* that makes them so mad!
For the English are all that a nation should be
And the flower of the English are Donald* and me!
   The English, the English, the English are best!
   I wouldn't give tuppence for all of the rest!

* *At this point the singer may substitute the name of the pianist.*

Lively ♩. = 76

mf

1. The rot-ten-est bits of these is-lands of ours We've
left in the hands of three un-friend-ly powers; Ex-a-mine the I-rish-man,

rit.

Welsh-man or Scot, You'll find he's a stin-ker as like-ly as not! The Eng-lish, the

Eng-lish, the Eng-lish are best! I would-n't give tup-pence for all of the rest!

80

Tonga

Oh it's hard to say, 'Hoolima Kittiluca Cheecheechee',
But in Tonga that means 'No'.
If I ever have the money
'Tis to Tonga I shall go,
For each lovely Tongan maiden there
Will gladly make a date,
And by the time she's said, 'Hoolima Kittiluca Cheecheechee',
It is usually too late.

If I e - ver have the mo-ney____ 'Tis to Ton - ga I shall go, For each love - ly Ton - gan mai - den there Will glad - ly make a date, And by the time she's said, "Hoolima Kittiluca Cheecheechee', It is u - sual - ly too late.

(spoken)

colla voce

Drawing by Edward Burra

The Lord Chamberlain's Regulations

I *Smoking Is Permitted*
Smoking is permitted in the auditorium,
So if you want to have a smoke and you've got the price
Just light it up and puff away to Paradise
Because smoking is permitted in the auditorium.

II *The Safety Curtain*
The safety curtain must be lowered in the presence of each audience.
The safety curtain must be raised in the presence of each audience.

III *The Public May Leave*
The public may leave at the end of each performance
By all the exit doors.
All gangways, passages and staircases must be kept entirely free
From chairs or any other obstructions.
The public may leave at the end of each performance
By all the exit doors
And all such doors must at that time be open.
Commissionaire, won't you see that they're all open—
They got to be open.

At a smoking pace ♩ = 132

2 voices

BOTH

Smok - ing is per - mit - ted in the au - di - to - ri - um, _____

Smok - ing is _____ per - mit - ted in _____ the au - di - to - ri - um, _____ Yes,

Smok - ing is _____ per - mit - ted in _____ the au - di - to - ri - um, _____ So if you

84

smok - ing is per - mit - ted in the au - di - tor - i - um, ___

want to have a smoke and you've got the price Just light it up and puff a - way to

___ Yes, smok - ing is per - mit - ted in the au - di - to - ri -

Pa - ra - dise Be - cause ___ smok - ing is ___ per - mit - ted in the au - di -

- um. ___

- to - ri - um. ___

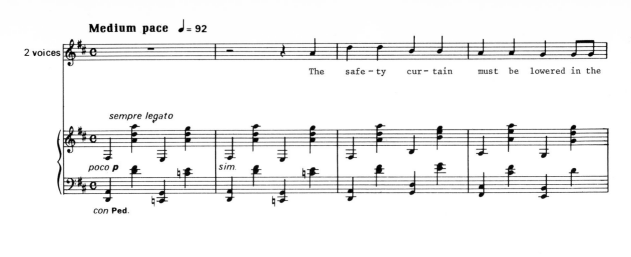

Medium pace ♩ = 92

2 voices

sempre legato

poco **p**

con **Ped.**

sim.

The safe-ty cur-tain must be lowered in the

pre-sence of each au-dience. _____ The safe-ty cur-tain

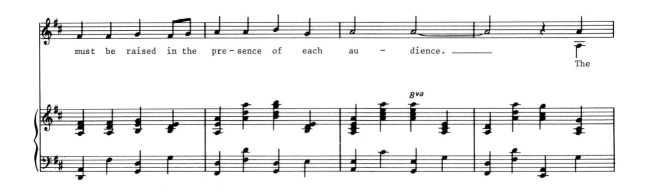

must be raised in the pre-sence of each au — dience. _____ The

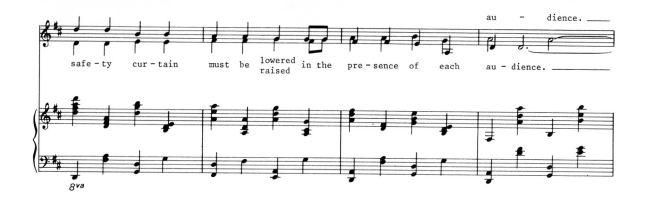

safe-ty cur-tain must be lowered/raised in the pre-sence of each au - dience. _____

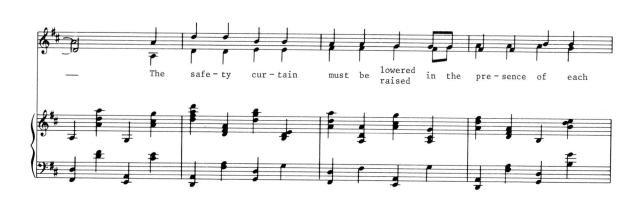

The safe-ty cur-tain must be lowered/raised in the pre-sence of each

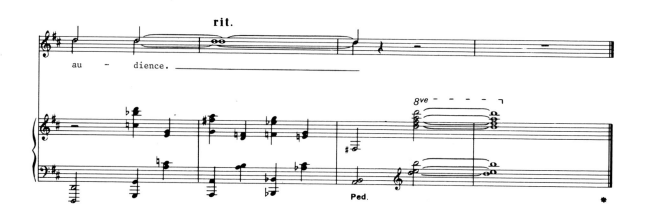

au - dience. _____

struc - tions. The pu-blic may leave at the end of each per-for-mance

By all the ex-it doors And all such doors must at that time be

o - pen. They got to be o - pen. Com-mis-sio-naire, won't you see that they're all

o - pen. They got to be o - pen. _____

"OH, MR. JONES, *WOULD* YOU WRITE SOME FUNNY LITTLE THING IN MY ALBUM?—

—AND IN MINE?—

—AND IN MINE?—

—AND IN MINE?—

—AND IN MINE?—

—AND IN MINE?—

—AND IN OURS?—

—HERE'S SOME INK—AND A PEN—

—AND A CHAIR—

—AND A TABLE—

—AND NOW WE'LL ALL GATHER ROUND, CHICKS AND BE READY FOR A REAL GOOD LAUGH!"

THE PROFESSIONAL HUMOURIST PAYS A VISIT

The Album

'Oh look at my album,'
The little girl said,
'The beautiful one I have bought;
Come write in my album, Tom, Harry and Ned,
Some fine and original thought.'
Tom took up a pencil and wrote
The following words I quote:
2 Ys U R, 2 Ys U B
I see you are too wise for me,
2 Ys U R, 2 Ys U B
You are too wise for me.

'How clever you are,
Did you write it yourself?'
Tom modestly made no reply.
The little girl turned to the others and said:
'Now Harry, come on, have a try.'
Then Harry gave Tom a quick look
And wrote in the back of the book:
By hook or by crook
I'll be last in this book.

'Oh Harry, oh Harry, how funny you are,'
Delighted, the little girl said,
'And now it's your turn.' She opened the page
And handed the album to Ned.
He carefully took up his pen
And wrote on the page there and then:
Roses are red, violets are blue,
Honey is sweet and so are you.
Roses are red, violets are blue,
Honey is sweet, like you.

'Oh Ned, you are naughty,'
The little girl cried
As she took back her album with care,
'Whenever I look at these words in the book
I'll think of the three of you there . . . singing:

2 Ys U R, 2 Ys U B
I C U R 2 Ys 4 me.
By hook or by crook
I'll be last in this book.
Roses are red, violets are blue
Honey is sweet and so are you.'

Lightly and freely ♩. = 80

1. 'Oh, look at my al-bum,' The lit-tle girl said, 'The
(2.) cle-ver you are, Did you write it your-self?' Tom
(3.) Har-ry, oh Har-ry, how fun-ny you are,' De-
(4.) Ned, you are naughty,' The lit-tle girl cried As she

beau-ti-ful one I have bought; Come write in my al-bum Tom, Har-ry and Ned Some
mo-dest-ly made no re-ply. The lit-tle girl turned to the o-thers and said: 'Now
-light-ed the lit-tle girl said. 'And now it's your turn.' She o-pened the page And
took back her al-bum with care, 'When-e-ver I look at these words in the book I'll

4th verse to CODA

fine and o-ri-gi-nal thought.' Tom took up a pen-cil and wrote _____ The
Har-ry, come on, have a try.' _____ Then Har-ry gave Tom a quick look _____ And
hand-ed the al-bum to Ned. _____ He care-ful-ly took up his pen _____ And
think of the three of you

94

Refrain 1 (TOM)

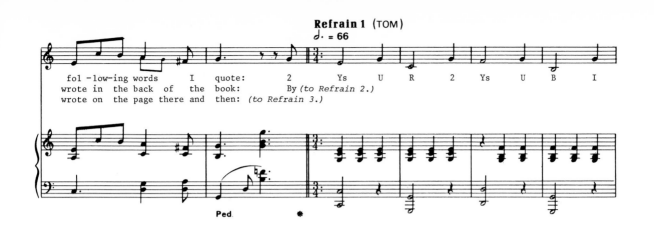

fol-low-ing words I quote: 2 Ys U R 2 Ys U B I
wrote in the back of the book: By *(to Refrain 2.)*
wrote on the page there and then: *(to Refrain 3.)*

see you are too wise for me, 2 Ys U R, 2

Ys U B, You are too wise for me. _____ 2

95

so are you. Ro - ses are red, vio - lets are blue,

Ho - ney is sweet, like you. _____ you. _____ 4.'Oh

1.   **2.**   **dal segno**

CODA (ALL THREE)

there .sing-ing 2 Ys U R 2 Ys U B I C U

Sing-ing by hook   or by crook   I'll be last _____

Ro - ses are red,   vio-lets are blue,   Ho - ney is

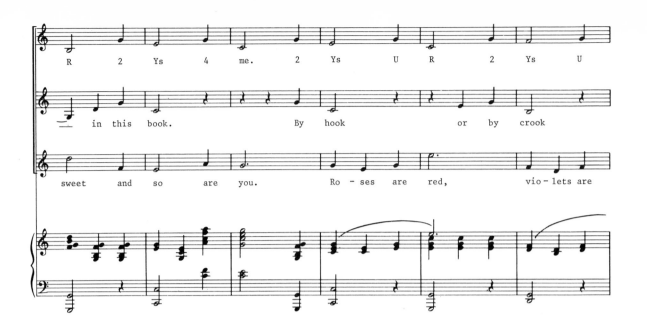

Song of Reproduction

I had a little gramophone;
I'd wind it round and round,
And with a sharpish needle
It made a cheerful sound.

And then they amplified it;
It was much louder then,
And you sharpened fibre needles
To make it soft again.

Today for reproduction
I'm as eager as can be;
Count me among the faithful fans
Of High Fidelity.

High Fidelity! Hi Fi's the thing for me—
With an L.P. disc and an F.M. set
And a corner reflex cabinet,
High Frequency range
And down with Auto-change!
All the highest notes, neither sharp nor flat:
The ear can't hear as high as that,
Still I ought to please any passing bat
With my High Fidelity.

*"A juke box would
make all the difference
to this place."*

Who made this circuit up for you anyway? I'm
surprised they let you have it in here! The
acoustics are all wrong. Raise the ceiling
four feet, put the fireplace from that wall to that
wall, and you'll still only get the stereophonic
effect if you sit in the bottom of that cupboard.
What a horrible shoddy job they've fobbed you
off with . . .! You've got your negative feedback
coupled in with your push-pull input-output; take
that across your red-head pickup to your tweeter,
and if you're modding more than eight you're
going to get wow on your top—try to bring that
down through your rumble filter to your woofer.
And what have you got?
Flutter on your bottom!

High Fidelity! F.F.R.R. for me!
I've an opera here that you shan't escape
On miles and miles of recording tape;
High decibel gain
Is easy to obtain;
With the tone control at a single touch
Bel Canto sounds like Double Dutch.
Then I never did care for music much—
It's High Fidelity!

(The middle section of the lyric is recited as a monologue)

wind it round and round, And with a shar-pish nee - dle It made a cheer-ful sound. And

then they am-pli-fied it; It was much lou-der then, And you shar-pened fi-bre nee-dles To

strongly, like a march

make it soft a-gain. To - day for re - pro-duc-tion I'm as ea-ger as can be; Count

slower   **Faster** ♩ = 100

me a-mong the faith-ful fans of High Fi-de-li-ty.   1. High Fi-de-li-ty!   Hi
                                                       2. High Fi-de-li-ty!   F.

101

Fi's the thing for me-
F. R. R. for me!

With an L. P. disc and an F. M. set And a
I've an o-pe-ra here that you shan't es-cape On

cor-ner re-flex ca-bi-net,
miles and miles of re-cord-ing tape;

High Fre-quen-cy range And down with Au-to-change! All the
High de-ci-bel gain Is ea-sy to ob-tain; With the

(spoken)

highest notes, neither sharp nor flat: The
tone con-trol at a single touch *Bel*

ear can't hear as high as that, Still I
Can - to sounds like Double Dutch— Then I

ought to please any passing bat With my High Fi-de-li-ty.
never did care for music much It's— High Fi-de-li-ty!

Ill Wind

(Mozart's Horn Concerto in E flat Koechel No. 495)

I once had a whim and I had to obey it
To buy a French Horn in a second-hand shop;
I polished it up and I started to play it
In spite of the neighbours who begged me to stop.

To sound my Horn, I had to develop my embouchure;
I found my Horn was a bit of a devil to play.

So artfully wound
To give you a sound,
A beautiful sound so rich and round.

Oh, the hours I had to spend
Before I mastered it in the end.

But that was yesterday and just today I looked in the usual place—
There was the case but the Horn itself was missing.

Oh, where can it have gone?
Haven't you—hasn't anyone seen my Horn?
Oh, where can it have gone?
What a blow! Now I know
I'm unable to play my Allegro.

Who swiped my Horn?
I'll bet you a quid
Somebody did,

(Drawing by Hoffnung)

103

Knowing I'd found a concerto and wanted to play it,
Afraid of my talent for playing the Horn.
Whoever it is I can certainly say it,
He'll probably wish he had never been born.

I've lost my Horn—I know I was using it yesterday.
I've lost my Horn, lost my Horn, found my Horn . . . gorn.
There's not much chance of getting it back though I'd willingly pay a reward.

I know some Hearty Folk whose party joke's
Pretending to hunt with the Quorn,
Gone away! Gone away! Was it one of them took it away?
Will you kindly return my Horn? Where is the devil who pinched that Horn?

I shall tell the Police I want my French Horn back.
I miss its music more and more and more.
Without the Horn I'm feeling sad and so forlorn.

I found a concerto, I wanted to play it,
Displaying my talent for playing the Horn,
But early today to my utter dismay it has totally vanished away.
I practised the Horn, then intended to play it but somebody took it away.
I practised the Horn and was longing to play it but somebody took it away.

My neighbour's asleep in his bed.
I'll soon make him wish he were dead.
I'll take up the Tuba instead!

Allegro vivace ♩.= 132

I once had a whim and I had to o-bey it To buy a French Horn in a sec-ond-hand shop; I po-lished it up and I star-ted to play it In spite of the neigh-bours who begged me to stop.

To sound my

105

Horn, __ I had to de-ve-lop my em-bou-chure, I found my Horn __ was a

bit of a de-vil to play. So art-ful-ly wound To give you a

sound, a beau-ti-ful sound so rich and round. Oh, _____ the

hours I had to spend Be-fore I mas-tered it in the end.

But that was yes-ter-day and just to-day I looked in the u-su-al place—

There was the case but the Horn it-self was mis-sing,

Oh, where can it have gone? ____ Have-n't you—has-n't a-ny-one seen my

Horn? Oh, where can it have gone? ____ What a blow! ____ Now I

know ____ I'm un - a - ble to play my Al - le - - gro.

Who swiped my Horn? I'll bet you a quid Some-bo - dy

did, Know-ing I'd found a con-cer-to and wan-ted to play it, A - fraid of my ta-lent for

play-ing the Horn, Who - ev - er it is I can cer-tain-ly say it, He'll pro - ba - bly wish he had

nev-er been born.

I've lost my

Horn ___ I know I was us-ing it yes-ter-day. I've lost my Horn,

lost my Horn, found my Horn... 'gorn'. There's

not much chance of get-ting it back though I'd wil-ling-ly pay a re-ward.

I know some Hear-ty Folk whose par-ty joke's Pre-ten-ding to hunt with the

Quorn, Gone a-way!___ Gone a-way!___ Was it one of them took it a-

-way? Will you kind-ly re-turn my

found a con-cer-to, I wan-ted to play it, Dis - play-ing my ta-lent for play-ing the Horn, But

ear-ly to-day to my ut - ter dis-may it has to-tal-ly va-nished a - way.

I

112

prac-tised the Horn, then in - ten-ded to play it but some-bo - dy took it a - way. _____ I

prac-tised the Horn and was long-ing to play it but some-bo - dy took it a - way.

My neigh-bour's a - sleep in his bed. I'll soon make him wish he were

dead. I'll take up the Tu - ba in - stead! wah! wah!

Guide to Britten

Who-oo-oo? Who-oo-oo is
Benjamin Britten?
Please don't send him up, again!

Edward Benjamin Britten,
Born Lowestoft, nineteen-thirteen;
That is, approximately.
Entered the Royal College of Music,
Studied under Frank Bridge
(According to Percy Scholes).
His work was soon in rehearsal
Because he always used . . . Purcell!

A rising young composer, he published every spring
An Olde English Folk Song for Peter Pears to sing.
The judges at each festival
Admired his *Sinfonietta*,
And voted it the best of all,
They'd never heard a better.
'Twas applauded by the masses,
The middle classes too,
And even by the Harewoods and the County Set,
Yes, even by the Doggy Doggy Few!

Art Songs! Quartets! Cantatas!
A *Spring Symphony* for Sackbut,
Psaltery, and Siffleur.
But this was not all! No!
Whenever he had a spare half hour,
It was always—*Let's make an Opera*!
Peter Grimes! Cribbed from Crabbe.
Peter Grimes! Sung all over the civilised world.
And in America.
Pierre Grimes! Pedro Grimo! Pyotr Grimsky!
Peter J. Grimes!

Of the first *Beggar's Opera* they used to say
That it made Gay rich, and it made Rich gay:
Revived by our hero after all these years,
It made Bundles for Britten and Piles for Pears.
The Rape of Lucretia was splendid fun
And night after night was discreetly done,
But best of them all we should like to state
Was the night when the curtain came down—too late!
His mother kept *Albert Herring* in curls,
He was never allowed to go out with girls.
His terrible fate he long endured
Until *Albert Herring* got Pickled and Cured.

Nor did Uncle Benjie forget the dear little children,
Composing for them
The Young Person's Guide to the Orchestra!
In which are explained the capabilities of each instrument,
Such as the Pianoforte . . .

You can play on the white notes . . .
You can play on the black notes . . .
You can screw up the stool . . .
Or you can screw it down
(The Turn of the Screw . . .)
You can raise the piano lid . . .
And you can shut it again . . .
So much for the Pianoforte!

But back to Opera and *Billy Budd*.
(Lyrics by Alan Melville):
With floggings and hangings and pitch and toss,
And nothing but men . . . Oh, it made Joan Cross!
As for *Gloriana* . . . !
As Covent Garden discovered all too soon!
You can pay John Piper
But you can't call the tune!
But *Gloriana* was a social success;
It turned out a regular Orgy . . . and Bess!

So Rule Britannia!
While Britten rules the staves,
All the music-loving public
Are his slaves!

amin Britten

115

up a-gain! Please don't send him up a-gain! Ed-ward Ben-ja-min Brit-ten,

Born Low-es-toft, nine-teen-thir-teen; That is, approximately. *(spoken)* En-tered the Roy-al Col-lege of Mu-sic,

Stu-died un-der Frank Bridge (Ac-cor-ding to Per-cy Scholes). His work was soon in re-

-hear-sal Be-cause he al-ways u-sed Pur-cell! A ri-sing young com-

Recit.

Risoluto ♩ = 116

Allegretto ♩ = 92

-po - ser, he pub-lished ev - ery spring ___ An Ol-de Eng-lish Folk Song for

Pe-ter Pears to sing. The ju-dges at each fes-ti-val Ad - mired his *Sin-fo* -

- *niet-ta*, And vo-ted it the best of all, They'd ne - ver heard a bet - -

- - - ter. 'Twas ap-plaud-ed by the mas - ses, The mid-dle clas-ses

Slower

too, _____ And ev-en by the Hare-woods and the Coun-ty Set, Yes,

ev-en by the Dog-gy, Dog-gy Few!

Recit.

(spoken)

Art Songs! Quartets! Cantatas!

A *Spring Symphony* for Sackbut, Psaltery, and Siffleur. But this was not all!

No! Whenever he had a spare half hour, It was always *Let's make an Opera!*

(Fog Horn) *(Fog Horn)* *(Fog Horn)*

Peter Grimes! Cribbed from Crabbe. *Peter Grimes!* Sung all over the

civilised world. And in America. Pier-re Grimes! Pe-dro Gri-mo! Pyo-tr Grim-sky! Pe-ter J. Grimes! __

first *Beg-gar's O - pera* they used to say That it made Gay rich
Rape of Lu - cre - tia was splen-did fun And night af - ter night
mo - ther kept *Al - bert Her - ring* in curls, He was ne - ver al - lowed

and it made Rich gay: Re - vived by our he - ro af - ter all these
was dis-creet-ly done, But best of them all we should like to
to go out with girls. His ter - ri - ble fate he long en -

years, It made Bun -dles for Brit-ten and Piles for
state Was the night when the cur - tain came down — too
- dured Un - til *Al - - bert Her - ring* got pick-led and

(elbows on black notes)

And you can shut it again..

So much for the Pianoforte! But back to
Opera and *Billy Budd*

♩ = 184

(Lyrics by Alan Melville):

With

mf

flog-gings and hang-ings and pitch and toss, And no-thing but men,

Oh, it made Joan Cross! As for *Glo* — — *ri-a-na...*

(spoken)

Gloriana!!

As Covent Garden discovered all
too soon, You can pay John Piper

But you can't call the tune!

8va bassa

122

Excelsior

Sherpa sir? Sherpa sir? Sherpa?
Everest, lady? Straight through the monastery
garden and first on the right—you can't miss it.

There's a little brown-eyed Sherpa to the north of Khatmandu
Who was with them when they made the great ascent;
'Tis a triumph that I share,
I can tell them: *I was there*!
But I couldn't be more sorry that I went.

It's all right for the Tiger of the Snows, the celebrated
Sherpa Tensing, otherwise known as Tensing Norky, or
Sirdar Bhotia Norky Tensing, or, as we call him in the
Khumbu, 'Fancy pants'. It's all right for him! He goes
up and down Everest like a yo-yo, or as you call it in
English, 'Lift'.

But I've no head for heights;
I can't sleep at nights;
It's been stark staring horror for me
1933 – 1935 – 1936 – 1938
1951 – 1952 – 1953! Oh . . .

Year after year, September or June,
Just at the end of the dreary monsoon,
A horrible rumour would run round the plain—
Everest calling Tensing again!

When Tensing hears Everest calling
He drags us up time after time;
Oh life in Nepal's been appalling
For Sherpas with no wish to climb.

Up we all go according to plan.
I have to carry the oxygen can.
With ice-falls to camp on and cramp in your crampon—
Everest calling Tensing again!

Sure enough this year he comes bouncing into the
village, shouting—'Everybody up Everest! Last
one up's a Sherpa!'

Camp One! No fun!
Camp Two! What to do?
Camp Three! Too high for me!
Up 9000 feet to Camp Four. Only 2000 feet more!
The Western Cwm! I want me moom!
The Lhotse! Oh, the pain in me tootsie!
The South Col! I'm very unwoll!
To the summit! No! I won't, dummit!

Yes Tensing hears Everest calling;
I bear him no malice for that,
Though he called me a twerp when I told him some Sherpas
Prefer it down here where it's flat—
And I might have cracked back,
'I'm a man, not a Yak'.
I'll tremble no more at that haunting refrain—
Everest calling Tensing again!

There's a broken-winded Sherpa who is back in Khatmandu;
As a climber he is just an also-ran,
And India and Nepal
Have no use for him at all—
Both try to palm him off on Pakistan.

So a frozen-footed Sherpa's on the Road to Mandalay
Though he knows the Himalayas back to front.
If you want a repetition
Of that sort of expedition—
You're a better man than I am,
Colonel Hunt!

Main Chorus only (the rest of this number was performed as monologue and recitative)

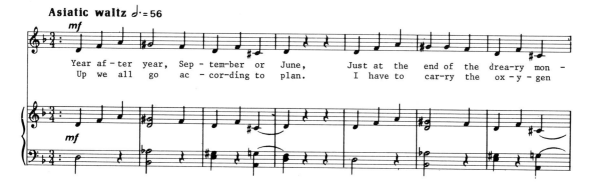

125

soon, A hor-ri-ble ru-mour would run round the plain — E - ver-est cal - ling
can. With ice-falls to camp on and cramp in your crampon —

Ten-sing a - gain! Oo _____ Hoo - ray! When Ten-sing hears E -ver-est

To last bar
(spoken)

cal-ling _____ He drags us up time af-ter time _____ And life in Ne -

-pal's been ap - pal-ling for Sher-pas with no wish to climb. - ray!

sf

The Bedstead Men

When you're walking in the country
Far from villages or towns,
When you're seven miles from nowhere and beyond,
In some dark deserted forest
Or a hollow of the Downs,
You may come across a lonely pool, or pond.
And you'll always find a big, brass, broken bedstead by the bank:
There's one in every loch and mere and fen.
Don't think it's there by accident,
It's us you have to thank:
The Society of British Bedstead Men.

   Oh the hammer ponds of Sussex
   And the dew ponds of the West
   Are part of Britain's heritage,
   The part we love the best;
   Every eel- and fish- and mill-pond
   Has a beauty all can share . . .
   But not unless it's got a big brass broken bedstead there!

127

So we filch them out of attics,
We beg them from our friends,
We buy them up in auction lots
With other odds and ends,
Then we drag them 'cross the meadows
When the moon is in the sky . . .
So watch the wall, my darling, while the Bedstead Men go by!

The League of British Bedstead Men
Is marching through the night,
A desperate and dedicated crew.
Under cover of the hedges,
Always keeping out of sight,
For the precious load of Bedsteads must get through!

The Society for Putting
Broken Bedsteads into Ponds
Has another solemn purpose to fulfil;
On our coastal sands and beaches
Or where waving willow wands
Mark the borders of a river, stream or rill,
You'll always find a single laceless left-hand leather boot:
A bootless British river bank's a shock.
We leave them there at midnight;
You can track a member's route,
By the alternating prints of boot and sock.

Oh the lily ponds of Suffolk
And the mill-ponds of the West
Are part of Britain's heritage,
The part we love the best;
Her river banks and sea-shores
Have a beauty all can share,
Provided there's at least one boot,
Three treadless tyres,
A half-eaten pork pie,
Some oil drums,
An old felt hat,
A lorry load of tarblocks
And a broken bedstead there!

Flowing ♩ = 126

mf

1. When you're walk-ing in the coun-try Far from
5. The So - ci - e - ty for Put-ting Bro-ken

vil - la - ges and towns, When you're se-ven miles from no-where and be - yond,
Bedsteads in - to ponds Has a - no-ther so - lemn pur-pose to ful-fil;

In some dark de - ser - ted fo - rest Or a hol-low of the Downs, You may
On our coastal sands and beaches Or where wav-ing wil-low wands Mark the

come a-cross a lone-ly pool, or pond. And you'll al-ways find a big brass bro - ken
borders of a ri - ver, stream or rill, You'll al-ways find a sin - gle lace-less

129

bed-stead by the bank: There's one in ev-ery loch and mere and fen. Don't
left-hand lea-ther boot: A boot-less Bri-tish ri-ver bank's a shock. We

think it's there by ac-ci-dent, It's us you have to thank: The So-ci-e-ty of Bri-tish Bed-stead
leave them there at mid-night; You can track a mem-ber's route By the al-ter-na-ting prints of boot and

Men. 2. Oh, the ham-mer ponds of Sus-sex And the dew ponds of the West Are
sock. 6. Oh, the li-ly ponds of Suf-folk And the mill-ponds of the West Are

2nd time to **CODA**

part of Bri-tain's he-ri-tage, The part we love the best; Ev-ery eel- and fish- and mill-pond Has a
part of Bri-tain's he-ri-tage, The part we love the best; Her ri-ver-banks and sea-shores Have a

rit. ... **a tempo**

beau-ty all can share...But not un-less it's got a big brass bro-ken bed-stead there!

3. So we filch them out of at-tics, We beg them from our friends, We

buy them up in auc-tion lots With o-ther odds and ends, Then we drag them 'cross the mea-dows When the

rit. ... **a tempo**

moon is in the sky... So watch the wall, my dar-ling, while the Bed-stead Men go by!

131

4. The League of Bri-tish Bed-stead Men Is march-ing through the night, A de-spe-rate and de-di-ca-ted crew. Un-der co-ver of the hed-ges, Al-ways keep-ing out of sight, For the pre-cious load of Bed-steads Must get through!

beau-ty all can share, Pro-vi-ded there's a boot, Pro-vi-ded there's a boot, Pro-

132

-vi-ded there's at least one boot,

(spoken) Three treadless tyres, A half-eaten pork pie, Some oil drums, An old felt hat, A lorry load of

ritenuto

ff

tarblocks And a bro-ken bed-stead there!

a tempo

allargando

ff

Ped.

Vanessa

I suffer in silence more than most—
I suppose I'm made that way,
But there comes a time when it's *talk* or *burst*!
That time has come today—
The most ghastly crisis of my whole life.
I don't want to be a bore
But it's time for chums to rally round.
I mean, that's what chums are for!
I said to myself when it happened: 'I—
I just can't face this thing alone;
I don't dare leave the house of course,
But, thank God, there's the phone.'
So I've spent today giving all my friends a ring
And tonight I'm facing one more, quite appalling thing.

Nobody wants to hear about Vanessa
And the terrible thing Vanessa's done to me!
I rang up good old Arthur
Before it got me down,
But his mother, Mrs Hapsburg,
Told me Arthur's out of town;
She obviously thought I was only trying to impress her,
When I said I needed Arthur right away—
And she didn't really seem to want to hear about Vanessa
And the vitally urgent thing I've got to say!

Nobody wants to hear about Vanessa
And the hideous mess Vanessa's got me in.
I got through to the Harts
And they were as nice as they could be,
But Siriol explained they'd got
John Cranko there to tea.
Sydney couldn't have been *toujours la politesse*-r
But he said he had to go out and hadn't shaved—
So there wasn't time to stay and hear me talk about Vanessa
And the quite fantastic way that she's behaved.

I rang up Ethel Seale in the middle of a meal;
She said she'd ring me back; I know she won't.
Virginia's gone to Cannes with that rather awful man;
God knows what she sees in him, I don't.
Henry wouldn't hear a word, he'd got something on the Third;
Then somebody rang me up—by mistake;
While Lucienne I think must have had too much to drink—
She kept mumbling on about Go and Jump in a Lake.

Anyway,
None of them wanted to hear about Vanessa
And the unforgivable treatment I've received.
Sandy isn't on the phone now,
So that goes for Julian too—
Peter Myers has had his cut off,
That's the best thing he could do!
I don't want to unburden myself to Janet, bless her.
And it isn't the sort of thing I discuss with Swann—
So I couldn't find a soul to hear me talk about Vanessa
And the quite impossible way she's carrying on!

Nobody wants to hear about Vanessa
And the indescribably awful thing she's done.
I rang up Elisabeth hourly,
And every time I tried,
Somebody took the receiver off,
But nobody replied.
When I think of the times I've acted as father confessor
When their permutated love lives go astray,
It's hard to find that not a single one of my so-called friends
Can spare a minute to listen to what I've got to say!

Perhaps *you*'d like to hear about Vanessa?
What she did—and how it's finished me because . . .
No! It's obvious all of you here just couldn't care less about Vanessa.
So I'm bothered if I'm going to tell you what it was!

(Main melody only. The music for the introduction verse was extemporised in performance.)

Allegro ♩ = 132

poco f

1. No - bo - dy wants to hear a - bout Va - nes - sa __ And the
2. No - bo - dy wants to hear a - bout Va - nes - sa __ And the
4. None of them wan-ted to hear a - bout Va - nes - sa __ And the
5. No - bo - dy wants to hear a - bout Va - nes - sa __ And the
6. -haps you'd like to hear a - bout Va - nes - sa?__ What she

poco f

Last time to CODA

ter - ri - ble thing Va - nes - sa's done to me! I
hi - de - ous mess Va - nes - sa's got me in. I
un - for gi - va - ble treat-ment I've re - ceived. etc.
in - de - scri - ba - bly aw - ful thing she's done etc.
did and how it's fi - nished me be - cause.. (to coda)

rang up good old Ar - thur Be - fore it got me down, But his
got through to the Harts And they were as nice as they could be But

mo - ther, Mrs - Haps - burg, Told me Ar - thur's out of town; She
Si - ri - ol ex - plained they'd got John Cran - ko there to tea. Syd - ney

136

ob - vious-ly thought I was on - ly try-ing to im - press her, _____ When I
could-n't have been *tou-jours la po - li - tesse*-r _____ But he

said I need - ed Ar-thur right a - way — And she did-n't real-ly seem to want to
said he had to go out and had - n't shaved — So there was-n't time to stay and hear me

hear a - bout Va-nes - sa And the vi-tal-ly ur - gent thing I'd got to say. _____
talk a - bout Va-nes - sa And the quite fan-tas - tic way that she's be - haved. _____

1. *repeat for verses 2,5,6* **2.** *(verse 3 only)*

(Verse 6 only) Per - 3. I rang up E - thel Seale in the

mid-dle of a meal; She said she'd ring me back; I know she won't. Vir-

- gi-nia's gone to Cannes with that ra-ther aw-ful man; God knows what she sees in him, I

R.H.

Free time   **a tempo**   **Da capo**

(spoken)

don't. Henry wouldn't hear a word, While Lucienne I think   4. Anyway,
he'd got something on the must have had too much
Third; Then somebody rang to drink   She kept
me up – by mistake; mumbling on about
Go and Jump in a   Lake.

✠ **CODA**

No! It's obvious all of you less about Vanessa. So I'm bothered if I'm going was!
here just couldn't care to tell you what it

sf   *sf*

8va   *8va*

138

Twice Shy

When a man comes bouncing into a pub
With a couple of girls in tow,
When he sets up a shout of 'Drinks all round
And a table for six please, Joe!'
When he kisses the barmaid,
Knocks down the dart-board,
Yells for the cabaret . . .
When you're wondering whether you might move on
Someone is sure to say:
   You know what his trouble is, don't you?
   He's shy.

  He's shy, he's shy,
  Though he wears a fluorescent tie.
  With a deep-down need to assert himself,
  We know the reason why:
  He's shy, he's shy—
  Give him another try:
  When you hear that voice in a crowded room
  And that laugh (Ha! Ha!) like a sonic boom,
  Go right on over to meet your doom
  'Cause underneath he's shy,
  He's really terribly shy.

When it's Ladies' Night at the Garrick Club
And a young woman comes in
Smoking a six-inch Burmah cheroot
And playing a violin;
When she slips off her sable,
Jumps on the table,
Asking 'Who wants a lark?'
Then the elderly member who signed her in
Will tentatively remark:
   'Of course she's just compensating for a deep, inborn lack of
   self-confidence: she's really a very shy person.'

  She's shy, she's shy,
  She's as sensitive as you or I.
  So sad she has to behave like this,
  It makes you want to cry.
  She's shy, she's shy,
  We know the reason why.
  Though she's published a book called *I Confess*
  And her private life is a public mess,
  Still she looks quite sweet in her topless dress,
  And underneath she's shy,
  She's really dreadfully shy!

139

Of course there are times when we're all ill at ease
Though we try to act suave and cool;
When everyone seems to know everyone else
And it feels like that first day at school.
It can be a nuisance
Affecting insouciance,
Trying to mix with the crowd:
Knowing one's talking just-that-little-bit-too-fast
And laughing a lot too loud . . .
    And of course the explanation for this is:

We're shy, we're shy,
You'll have spotted it with half an eye;
And it does no good to conceal that fact,
It's useless to deny:
He's shy, *I'm* shy,
However hard we try:
Though we've got the music and words off pat,
Every single time that we Drop Our Hat
We can't help wondering what we're at—
'Cause underneath we're shy,
We're really terribly SHY!

140

'Drinks all round And a ta-ble for six please, Joe!,' When he kis-ses the bar-maid.
Bur-mah che-root And play-ing a vi - o - lin; When she slips off her sa - ble,
eve - ry-one else And it feels like that first day at school. It can be a nui-sance Af-

knocks down the dart-board, Yells for the ca - ba - ret... When you're won-der-ing whether you
Jumps on the ta - ble, Ask-ing 'Who wants a lark?,' Then the el-der-ly mem-ber who
-fect - ing in-sou-ciance, Try-ing to mix with the crowd: Know - ing one's talking just that

rit.

a tempo, but now easier

mp

might move on Some-one is sure to say: He's shy, he's
signed her in Will ten-ta-tive-ly 're - mark: She's shy, she's
lit-tle bit too fast And laugh-ing a lot too loud... We're shy, we're

8va

mp

Ped. *

shy, Though he wears a flu-o - re-scent tie. He has this need to as -
shy, She's as sen-si-tive as you or I. So sad she has to be -
shy, You'll have spot-ted it with half an eye; And it does no good to con-

141

-sert him-self, We know the rea-son why: He's shy, he's shy —
-have like this, It makes you want to cry. She's shy, she's shy —
-ceal that fact, It's use-less to de-ny: We're shy, we're shy —

Give him a-no-ther try: When you hear that voice in a crow-ded room And that
We know the rea-son why. Though she's pub-lished a book called *I Con-fess* And her
How ev-er hard we try: Though we've got the mu-sic and words off pat, Ev-ery

laugh(Ha! Ha!)like a so-nic boom, Go right on o-ver to meet your doom 'Cause
pri-vate life is a pub-lic mess,Still she looks quite sweet in her top-less dress, And
sin-gle time that we Drop Our Hat We can't help won-der-ing what we're at — 'Cause

un - der-neath he's shy, He's real-ly ter-ri-bly shy.
un - der-neath she's shy, She's real-ly ter-ri-bly shy.
un - der-neath we're shy, We're real-ly ter-ri-bly shy.

Have Some Madeira, M'dear

She was young! She was pure! She was new! She was nice!
She was fair! She was sweet seventeen!
He was old! He was vile and no stranger to vice!
He was base! He was bad! He was mean!
   He had slyly inveigled her up to his flat
   To see his collection of stamps,
   And he said as he hastened to put out the cat,
   The wine, his cigar and the lamps:

'Have some Madeira, m'dear!
You really have nothing to fear;
I'm not trying to tempt you—it wouldn't be right.
You shouldn't drink spirits at this time of night;
Have some Madeira, m'dear!
It's very much nicer than Beer;
I don't care for Sherry, one cannot drink Stout,
And Port is a wine I can well do without;
It's simply a case of *Chacun à son GOUT!*
Have some Madeira, m'dear!'

Unaware of the wiles of the snake in the grass,
Of the fate of the maiden who topes,
She lowered her standards by raising her glass,
Her courage, her eyes—and his hopes.
   She sipped it, she drank it, she drained it, she did;
   He quietly refilled it again
   And he said as he secretly carved one more notch
   On the butt of his gold-handled cane:

'Have some Madeira, m'dear!
I've got a small cask of it here,
And once it's been opened you know it won't keep.
Do finish it up—it will help you to sleep;
Have some Madeira, m'dear!
It's really an excellent year;
Now if it were Gin, you'd be wrong to say yes,
The evil Gin does would be hard to assess
(Besides, it's inclined to affect m' prowess!)
Have some Madeira, m'dear!'

Then there flashed through her mind what her mother had said
With her antepenultimate breath:
'Oh, my child, should you look on the wine when it's red
Be prepared for a fate worse than death!'
    She let go her glass with a shrill little cry.
    Crash, tinkle! It fell to the floor.
    When he asked: 'What in heaven . . .?' she made no reply,
    Up her mind and a dash for the door.

'Have some Madeira, m'dear!'
Rang out down the hall loud and clear.
A tremulous cry that was filled with despair,
As she paused to take breath in the cool midnight air;
'Have some Madeira, m'dear!'
The words seemed to ring in her ear
Until the next morning she woke up in bed,
With a smile on her lips and an ache in her head—
And a beard in her earhole that tickled and said:
'Have some Madeira, m'dear!'

Fast waltz ♩. = 76

She was young! She was pure! She was new! She was
Un-a-ware of the wiles of the snake in the

nice! She was fair! She was sweet se-ven-teen! _____ He was old! He was
grass, Of the fate of the mai-den who topes, _____ She low-ered her

vile and no stran-ger to vice! He was base! He was bad! He was mean!
stan-dards by rais-ing her glass, Her_ cou-rage, her eyes—and his hopes.

Ped.   *

145

He had sly-ly in-vei-gled her up to his flat To see his col -
She sipped it, she drank it, she drained it, she did; He quiet-ly re -

- lec-tion of stamps,
-filled it a - gain
And he said as he hast-ened to put out the
And he said as he se-cret-ly carved one more

poco rit.   a tempo

cat, The wine, his ci-gar and the lamps:
notch On the butt of his gold-hand-led cane:

Have some Ma -

- dei-ra, m' dear!
You real-ly have no-thing to fear;
I've got a small cask of it here,

I'm not trying to tempt you—it would-n't be right. You should-n't drink
And once it's been o - pened you know it won't keep. Do fi - nish it

spi-rits at this time of night;
up— it will help you to sleep;
Have some Ma - dei-ra, m' dear!

It's ve - ry much ni - cer than Beer:
It's real-ly an ex - cel-lent year;
I don't care for
Now if it were

Sher-ry, one can-not drink Stout, And Port is a wine I can well do with-
Gin you'd be wrong to say yes, The e - vil Gin does would be hard to as -

out; It's sim-ply a case of *Cha - cun à son GOUT!*
sess (Be - sides, it's in - clined to af - fect m' prow - ess!) Have some Ma-

- dei - ra, m' dear!'   dear!'

agitato

Then there flashed through her

mind what her mo-ther had said With her an - te - pe - nul - ti - mate breath:

'Oh, my child, should you look on the wine when it's red Be pre - pared for a

più mosso

fate worse than death!' She let go her glass with a shrill lit - tle

cry. Crash, tin - kle! It fell to the floor. When he asked: 'What in

Ped. *

hea-ven..? She made no re - ply, Up her mind and a dash for the door. _____

149

Meno mosso

Un - til the next morn - ing she woke up in bed, With a smile on her

Tempo primo

lips and an ache in her head — And a beard in her ear - hole that

ti - ckled and said: *(spoken)* 'Have some Ma - dei - ra, m' dear!'

151

The Armadillo

I was taking compass bearings for the Ordnance Survey
By an Army Training Camp on Salisbury Plain;
I had packed up my theodolite, was calling it a day,
When I heard a voice that sang a sad refrain:

     'Oh my darling Armadillo
     Let me tell you of my love,
     Listen to my Armadillo roundelay.
     Be my fellow on my pillow
     Underneath this weeping willow,
     Be my darling Armadillo all the day.'

I was somewhat disconcerted by this curious affair
For a single Armadillo, you will own,
On Salisbury Plain, in summer, is comparatively rare
And a pair of them is practically unknown.

     Drawn by that mellow solo
     There I followed on my bike
     To discover what these Armadillo
     Lovers would be like:

'Oh my darling Armadillo,
How delightful it would be
If for us these silver wedding bells would chime;
Let the orange blossom billow,
You need only say 'I will'—oh,
Be my darling Armadillo all the time.'

Then I saw them, in a hollow, by a yellow muddy bank—
One Armadillo singing . . . to an armour-plated Tank!
Should I tell him? Gaunt and rusting, with the willow tree above,
This—abandoned on manoeuvres—is the object of your love!

I left him to his singing,
Cycled home without a pause.
Never tell a man the truth
About the one that he adores!

On the breeze that follows sunset
I could hear that sad refrain
Singing willow, willow, willow down the way,
And I seem to hear it still. Oh,
Vive l'amour, vive L'Armadillo!
'Be my darling Armadillo all the day.'

A tender moderato ♩ = 120

mp

I was ta-king com-pass bear-ings for the Or-dn-ance Sur-vey By an Ar-my Train-ing Camp on Salis-bury Plain; I had packed up my the-o-do-lite, was cal-ling it a day, When I

154

heard a voice that sang a sad re - frain: 'Oh my

Meno mosso ♩ = 96

dar-ling Ar-ma-dil-lo Let me tell you of my love, Lis-ten to my Ar-ma-dil-lo roun-de-

- lay Be my fel-low on my pil-low Un-der-neath this weep-ing wil-low, Be my

Tempo I

dar-ling Ar-ma-dil-lo all the day.'

155

I was some-what dis-con-cer-ted by this cu-ri-ous af-fair For a

sin-gle Ar-ma-dil-lo, you will own, On Salis-bury Plain, in sum-mer, is com-

-pa-ra-tive-ly rare And a pair of them is prac-ti-cal-ly un-known. Drawn

by that mel-low so-lo There I fol-lowed on my bike .To dis-co-ver what these Ar-ma-dil-lo

rit.   **Meno mosso**

Lo-vers would be like: 'Oh my dar-ling Ar-ma-dil-lo, How de-light-ful it would be If for

cresc.   *dim.*

us these sil-ver wed-ding bells would chime; Let the or-ange blos-som bil-low, You need

8va

f *ff* QUASI BELLS *(f)* . . . . *dim.*

Ped.   *

mp   *(dramatic recitation)*

on-ly say 'I will'-oh, Be my dar-ling Ar-ma-dil-lo all the time.'   Then I

colla voce **mp**

saw them, in a hollow, by a yellow muddy bank— One Armadillo singing...to an armour-plated Tank!

Quite quickly

poco cresc.

157

Middle tempo ♩= 112

Should I tell him? Gaunt and rusting, with the

willow tree above, This— a - bandoned on manoeuvres— is the   object of your love!

rit.   **Meno mosso** ♩= 96

I   left   him   to   his sing-ing,   Cy - cled

home with-out a pause...Ne-ver tell a man the truth A - bout the   one that he a - dores!   On the

(spoken)

breeze that follows sunset I could hear that sad refrain Sing-ing wil-low, wil-low, wil-low down the way, And I seem to hear it still. Oh, vive l'a - mour, vive l'Ar-ma - dil-lo 'Be my darling Ar-ma-dil-lo all the day, Be my dar-ling Ar - ma - dil-lo all the day.'

The Elephant

An Elephant's life is tedious, laborious and slow;
I've been an elephant all me life so I blooming well ought to know.

He never forgets a name or face,
He knows his way from place to place,
Remembers to be dutiful
And when to push and when to pull,
And when he's dead the dealer calls
And buys his tusks for billiard balls,
And all because an elephant's got a perfect memory.
That wasn't the life for me!

So I'm suffering from Amnesia,
My mind's a perfect blank!
Now life is very much easier—
Amnesia's to thank;
I'm being psychoanalysed,
I lie on a divan
And flap me ears and try to look
As barmy as I can.

I'm an Introverted Elephocentric Hypochondriac,
And I'll stick in the Elephants' nursing home
Till I get me memory back!

I'm suffering from Hysteria;
I nearly split me sides,
To watch the others get wearier
Of giving the children rides;
I've told my psychoanalyst
That I'm a Sacred Cow;
I'd like to carry a Howdah
But I can't remember how.

I'm an Introverted Elephocentric Hypochondriac,
And I'll stick in the Elephants' nursing home
Till I get me memory back!

I suffer from Schizophrenia—
It comes on me in spells;
Sometimes I'm King of Armenia,
At others I'm Orson Welles.
I tell them I'm Napoleon
And all that sort of bunk;
They never guess that all the time
I'm laughing up me trunk.

I'm an Introverted Elephocentric Hypochondriac,
And I'll stick in the Elephants' nursing home
Till I get me memory back!

te - di-ous, la - bo - ri-ous and slow; I've been an el - e-phant all me life so I

bloom-ing well ought to know. ____ He ne-ver for-gets a

name or face, oooh! ____ He knows his way from place to place,

oooh! ____ Re - mem-bers to be du - ti-ful And when to push and

when to pull, And when he's dead the dealer calls And buys his tusks for bil-liard balls,

largamente

(spoken)
Ooo _____ ooh! And all be-cause an el-e-phant's got a per-fect me-mo-

subito animato   **Allegretto scherzando** ♩=104

- ry.   That was-n't the life for me!   2.So I'm suf-fer-ing from Am - ne - si-a, My
(2.) suf-fer-ing from Hys - te - ri-a; I
(3.) suf-fer from Schi - zo - phre-ni-a— It

mind's a per-fect blank!   Now life is ve-ry much ea - si-er— Am - ne - si-a's to
near-ly split me sides,   To watch the o-thers get wear-i-er Of giv-ing the chil-dren
comes on me in spells;   Some-times I'm King of Ar - me-ni-a, At o thers I'm Or - son

thank; I'm be - ing psy - cho - an - a - lysed, I lie on a di - van And
rides; I've told my psy - cho - an - a - lyst_ That I'm a Sa - cred Cow; I'd
Welles. I tell them I'm Na - po - le - on_ And all that sort of bunk; They

poco rit. e cresc. _a tempo_

flap me ears and try to look As bar - my as_ I can. I'm an In - tro - ver - ted
like to car - ry a How - dah but I can't re - mem - ber how. I'm an In - tro - ver - ted
nev - er guess that all the time I'm laugh - ing up_ me trunk. I'm an In - tro - ver - ted

El - e - pho - cen - tric Hy - po - chon - dri - ac, And I'll stick in the El - e - phants' nur - sing home Till I
El - e - pho - cen - tric Hy - po - chon - dri - ac, And I'll stick in the El - e - phants' nur - sing home Till I
El - e - pho - cen - tric Hy - po - chon - dri - ac, And I'll stick in the El - e - phants' nur - sing home Till I

1.

get me mem - o - ry back! 3. I'm
get me mem - o - ry back! 4. I
get me mem - o - ry

The Gnu

A year ago last Thursday I was strolling in the zoo
When I met a man who thought he knew the lot;
He was laying down the law about the habits of Baboons
And the number of quills a Porcupine has got.
I asked him: 'What's that creature there?' He answered:
                                    'H'it's a H'elk'.
I might have gone on thinking that was true,
If the animal in question hadn't put that chap to shame
And remarked: 'I h'aint a H'elk. I'm a G-nu!

    I'm a G-nu, I'm a G-nu,
    The g-nicest work of g-nature in the zoo!
    I'm a G-nu, how do you do?
    You really ought to k-now w-ho's w-ho.
    I'm a G-nu, spelt G.N.U.,
    I'm g-not a Camel or a Kangaroo,
    So let me introduce,
    I'm g-neither Man nor Moose,
    Oh, g-no, g-no, g-no, I'm a G-nu!'

I had taken furnished lodgings down at Rustington-on-Sea
(Whence I travelled on to Ashton-under-Lyme)
And the second night I stayed there, I was wakened from a dream
Which I'll tell you all about some other time.
Among the hunting trophies on the wall above my bed,
Stuffed and mounted, was a face I thought I knew.
A Bison? An Okapi? Could it be . . . a Hartebeeste?
Then I seemed to hear a voice: 'I'm a G-nu!

      I'm a G-nu, a g-nother G-nu,
      I wish I could g-nash my teeth at you!
      I'm a G-nu, how do you do?
      You really ought to k-now w-ho's w-ho.
      I'm a G-nu, spelt G.N.U.,
      Call me Bison or Okapi and I'll sue!
      G-nor am I in the least
      Like that dreadful Hartebeeste,
      Oh, g-no, g-no, g-no, I'm a G-nu!'

year ago last Thursday I was   strolling in the zoo   When I   met a man who thought he knew the
taken furnished lodgings down at   Rustington-on-Sea,   (Whence I   travelled on to Ash-ton-under-

lot;   He was laying down the law about the habits of Baboons And the
- Lyme) And the second night I stayed there I was wakened from a dream Which I'll

number of quills a Porcupine has got.   I asked him: 'What's that creature there?' He
tell you all a-bout some other time.   A-mong the hunting trophies on the

answered: 'H'it's a H'elk.' I might have gone on thinking that was true,   If the
wall above my bed, Stuffed and mounted, was a face I thought I knew.   A

rit.

animal in question hadn't put that chap to shame And remarked: 'I h'aint a H'elk. I'm a G-
Bison? An Okapi? could it be...... a Hartebeeste? Then I seemed to hear a voice: I'm a G-

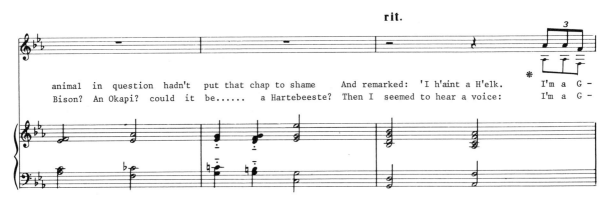

❋ *The initial G is pronounced throughout in all words.*

a tempo

-nu. I'm a G - nu, I'm a G - nu, The g-
-nu. I'm a G - nu, a g-noth-er G - nu, I

-ni - cest work of g-na-ture in the zoo!
wish I could g-nash my teeth at you! I'm a G - nu, how do you

do? You real - ly ought to k-now w-ho's w - ho. I'm a G-

- nu, Spelt G. N. U., I'm g-not a Ca-mel or a Kan - ga-
Call me Bi - son or O-ka - pi and I'll

169

-roo, So let me in-tro-duce, I'm g - nei-ther Man or Moose Oh, g-
sue! G-nor am I in the least Like that dread-ful Har - te-beest

-no, g-no, g-no, I'm a G - nu!" -no, g-no, g-no, I'm a G-

-nu! g - no, g-no, g-no, I'm a G - nu g-

-no, g-no, g-no, I'm a G - nu!

170

The Hippopotamus

A bold Hippopotamus was standing one day
On the banks of the cool Shalimar.
He gazed at the bottom as it peacefully lay
By the light of the evening star.
Away on a hilltop sat combing her hair
His fair Hippopotamine maid;
The Hippopotamus was no ignoramus
And sang her this sweet serenade:

    Mud, mud, glorious mud,
    Nothing quite like it for cooling the blood!
    So follow me, follow,
    Down to the hollow
    And there let us wallow
    In glorious mud!

The fair Hippopotama he aimed to entice
From her seat on that hilltop above,
As she hadn't got a ma to give her advice,
Came tiptoeing down to her love.
Like thunder the forest re-echoed the sound
Of the song that they sang as they met.
His inamorata adjusted her garter
And lifted her voice in duet:

    Mud, mud, glorious mud,
    Nothing quite like it for cooling the blood!
    So follow me, follow,
    Down to the hollow
    And there let us wallow
    In glorious mud!

Now more Hippopotami began to convene
On the banks of that river so wide.
I wonder now what am I to say of the scene
That ensued by the Shalimar side?
They dived all at once with an ear-splitting splosh
Then rose to the surface again,
A regular army of Hippopotami
All singing this haunting refrain:

    Mud, mud, glorious mud,
    Nothing quite like it for cooling the blood!
    So follow me, follow,
    Down to the hollow
    And there let us wallow
    In glorious mud!

Heavily, in the region of ♩. = 58

1. A bold Hip-po-po-ta-mus was stand-ing one
(2.) fair Hip-po-po-ta-ma he aimed to en-
(3.) more Hip-po-po-ta-mi be-gan to con-

day On the banks of the cool Sha-li-mar. He gazed at the bottom as it
-tice From her seat on that hill-top a-bove, As she had-n't got a ma to
-vene On the banks of that ri-ver so wide. I won-der now what am I to

peace-ful-ly lay By the light of the e-ven-ing star. _____ A-way on the
give her ad-vice, Came tip-toe-ing down to her love. _____ Like thun-der the
say of the scene That en-sued by the Sha-li-mar side? _____ They dived all at

hill top sat comb-ing her hair His fair Hip-po-po-ta-mine maid; _____ The
fo-rest re-e-choed the sound Of the song that they sang as they met. _____ His
once with an ear-split-ting splosh Then rose to the sur-face a-gain, _____ A

Hip-po-po - ta-mus was no ig-no-ra-mus And sang her this sweet se - re - nade: _____
i - na-mo - ra-ta ad - jus-ted her gar-ter And lif-ted her voice in du - et: _____
re - gu - lar ar-my of Hip-po-po - ta-mi All sing-ing this haunt-ing re - frain: _____

REFRAIN

Mud, mud, glo-ri - ous mud, Noth-ing quite like it for cool-ing the blood! So

1 and 2

fol-low me, fol-low, down to the hol-low And there let us wal-low In glo - - ri - ous

3. last time
rit.

mud! _____
2. The
3. Now glo - - ri - ous mud! _____

mf

The Ostrich

'Peek-a-boo, I can't see you—
Everything must be grand!
Boo-ka-pee, they can't see me
As long as I've got me head in the sand.
Peek-a-boo, it may be true—
There's something in what you've said
But we've got enough troubles in everyday life—
I just bury me head!'

'Oh Ostrich consider how the world we know
Is trembling on the brink.
Have you heard the news? May I hear your views?
Will you tell me what you think?'
The Ostrich lifted his head from the sand
About an inch or so:
'You will please excuse but disturbing news
I have no wish to know.

Oh, Peek-a-boo, I can't see you—
Everything must be grand!
Boo-ka-pee, they can't see me
As long as I've got me head in the sand.
Peek-a-boo, it may be true—
There's something in what you've said
But we've got enough troubles in everyday life—
I just bury me head!'

Then I noticed suddenly where we were;
I saw what time it was.
'Make haste', I said, 'it'll be too late;
We must leave this place because . . .'
He stuffed his wing-tips into his ears,
He would not hear me speak;
And back in the soft Saharan sand
He plunged his yellow beak.

'Oh, Peek-a-boo, I can't see you—
Everything must be grand!
Boo-ka-pee, they can't see me
As long as I've got me head in the sand.
Peek-a-boo, it may be true—
There's something in what you've said
But we've got enough troubles in everyday life—
I just bury me . . .' (*Loud explosion*)

From a sheltered oasis a mile away
I observed that dreadful scene
And a single plume came floating down
Where my Ostrich friend had been,
Because he would not hear those words,
Those words I had left unsaid:
'Here in this Nuclear Testing Ground
Is no place to bury your head!'

REFRAIN

Slyly ♩· = 76

'Peek - a - boo, I can't see you Eve-ry-thing must be grand! Boo - ka - pee, they

can't see me As long as I've got me head in the sand. Peek - a - boo, it may be true There's

some-thing in what you've said But we've got e-nough trou-bles in eve-ry - day life ——

Third time omit the next 17 bars to ⊕

♩ = 132

I just bu-ry me head!

1. 'Oh Os-trich con-si-der how the world we know Is
2. Then I no-ticed sud-den-ly where we were; I

✳ *At the end of the 3rd refrain this last bar should be drowned by a loud explosion. If no explosion is available, the pianist might lean on the piano keys with the length of his forearms.*

trem - bling on the brink. Have you heard the news? May I hear your views? Will you
saw what time it was. 'Make haste', I said, 'it'll be too late; We must

tell me what you think?' The Os - trich lift-ed his head from the sand, A -
leave this place be - cause....' He stuffed his wing - tips in - to his ears, He

- bout an inch or so: 'You will please ex - cuse but dis - tur - bing news I
would not hear me speak; And back in the soft Sa - ha - ran sand He

Da capo

have no wish to know. Oh,
plunged his yel - low beak. Oh,

attacca Verse 3

Ped.

178

Last time only Slow

3. From a shel-tered o - a - sis a mile a - way I ob-served that dread-ful

scene And a sin - gle plume came float-ing down Where my Os-trich friend had

been, Be - cause he would not hear those words, Those words I had left un -

Still slower   **rall.**

said: 'Here in this Nu - clear Tes-ting Ground is no place to bu - ry your head!'

Ped.   *

179

The Rhinoceros

Oh, nobody loves the Rhinoceros much—
If you ask the reason why,
They will tell you because of his scaly touch
Or his hard and glittering eye;
But should you ask a truthful man
You will get this quick response:
'I do not trust that thing on his nose,
The Bodger on his Bonce!'

Oh, the Bodger on the Bonce!
The Bodger on the Bonce!
Oh, pity the poor old Rhino with
The Bodger on the Bonce!

Yet a sensitive heart the Rhinoceros owns;
If you doubt it, here's the proof:
That thing on his nose is for taking stones
Out of a horse's hoof.
He seldom, if ever, meets a horse
(It is this that makes him sad)—
When he does then it hasn't a stone in its hoof,
But he would if he did and it had!

Oh, the Bodger on the Bonce!
The Bodger on the Bonce!
Oh, pity the poor old Rhino with
The Bodger on the Bonce!

And just to bring pleasure to those who like
To enjoy the natural scene,
He picks up litter on his spike
To keep the forest clean.
And if one day to his habitat
For a picnic you should roam,
He will open a tin should you have left
Your opener at home.

With the Bodger on the Bonce!
The Bodger on the Bonce!
Oh, pity the poor old Rhino with
The Bodger on the Bonce!

So treat the Rhinoceros as your friend
Though he looks a fearsome sight;
He amply justifies his end
Because his means are right;
And ask yourself, would *you* do as well
Fulfilling long-felt wants,
If Nature had endowed you with
A Bodger on your Bonce?

Yes, a Bodger on your Bonce!
A Bodger on your Bonce!
If Nature had endowed you with
A Bodger on your Bonce!

Bouncing, in the region of ♩. = 96

1. Oh,

no - bo - dy loves the Rhi - no - ce - ros much — If you ask the rea - son
(2.) sen - si - tive heart the Rhi - no - ce - ros owns; If you doubt it, here's the
(3.) just to bring plea - sure to those ___ who like To en - joy the nat - ural
(4.) treat the Rhi - no - ce - ros as ___ your friend Tho' he looks a fear - some

why,   They will tell you be - cause of his sca - ly touch Or his
proof: That thing on his nose is for ta - king stones
scene,   He picks ___ up lit - ter on his spike To
sight;   He am - ply jus - ti - fies his end Be -

hard and glit-tering eye; ___ But should you ask a truth - ful man You will
Out of a hor - se♭ hoof. ___ He sel-dom, if ev - er, meets a horse (It is
keep the fo - rest clean. ___ And if one day to his ha - bi✝tat For a
-cause his means are right; ___ And ask your-self, would *you* do as well Ful-

rit.

get this quick re - sponse: ___ 'I do not trust that thing on his nose, The
this that makes him sad) ___ When he does then it has-n't a stone in it s hoof, But he
pic - nic you should roam, ___ He will o - pen a tin should you have left Your
-fil - ling long felt wants, ___ If na - ture had en - dowed you with A

The Sloth

A Bradypus or Sloth am I,
I live a life of ease,
Contented not to do or die
But idle as I please;
I have three toes on either foot
Or half-a-doz on both;
With leaves and fruits and shoots to eat
How sweet to be a Sloth.

The world is such a cheerful place
When viewed from upside down;
It makes a rise of every fall,
A smile of every frown;
I watch the fleeting flutter by
Of butterfly or moth
And think of all the things I'd try
If I were not a Sloth.

184

I could climb the very highest Himalayas,
Be among the greatest ever tennis players,
Always win at chess or marry a princess or
Study hard and be an eminent professor,
I could be a millionaire, play the clarinet,
Travel everywhere,
Learn to cook, catch a crook,
Win a war, then write a book about it,
I could paint a Mona Lisa,
I could be another Caesar,
Compose an oratorio that was sublime:
The door's not shut
On my genius but
I just don't have the time!

For days and days among the trees
I sleep and dream and doze,
Just gently swaying in the breeze
Suspended by my toes;
While eager beavers overhead
Rush through the undergrowth,
I watch the sky beneath my feet—
How sweet to be a Sloth.

1. A Bra - dy - pus or Sloth am I, I live a life of ease,
(2) world is such a cheer - ful place When viewed from up - side down,
(4.) days and days a - mong the trees I sleep and dream and doze,

Con - ten - ted not to do or die But i - dle as I please;
It makes a rise of ev - ery fall, A smile of ev - ery frown;
Just gen - tly sway - ing in the breeze Sus - pen - ded by my toes;

— I have three toes on ei - ther foot Or half a doz on both;
— I watch the fleet - ing flut - ter by Of but - ter - fly or moth
— While ea - ger bea - vers o - ver - head Rush through the un - der - growth,

With leaves and fruits and shoots to eat How sweet to be a Sloth.
And think of all the things I'd try If
I watch the sky be - neath my feet— How

186

2. The I were not a Sloth. *(to 3.)* sweet *(whistle)* to be *(whistle)* a

Last time
meno mosso

rit. **Fine** | *più f*

Sloth. 3. I could climb the ve-ry high-est Hi-ma-la-yas, Be a-mong the great-est-

✳ *cantabile*

ev-er ten-nis-play-ers, Al-ways win at chess or mar-ry a prin-cess or Stu-dy hard and be an

e - mi - nent pro - fes-sor, I could be a mil-lion-aire, play the cla - ri - net,

✳ *A second singer or choir should whistle the right hand melody for the next 31 bars.*

Tra-vel ev-ery-where, Learn to cook, catch a crook, Win a war, then

write a book a-bout it, I could paint a Mo - na Li - sa, I could be a-no-ther

Cae - sar, Com-pose an o - ra - to - ri - o that was su - blime: The

Da capo al 𝄋

door's not shut On my ge - nius but I just don't have the time! 4. For

188

The Spider

I have fought a grizzly bear,
Tracked a cobra to its lair,
Killed a crocodile who dared to cross my path;
But the thing I really dread
When I've just got out of bed
Is to find that there's a spider in the bath.

I've no fear of wasps or bees,
Mosquitos only tease,
I rather like a cricket on the hearth;
But my blood runs cold to meet
In pyjamas and bare feet
With a great big hairy spider in the bath.

I have faced a charging bull in Barcelona,
I have dragged a mountain lioness from her cub,
I've restored a mad gorilla to its owner
But I don't dare to face that Tub . . .

What a frightful-looking beast—
Half an inch across at least—
It would frighten even Superman or Garth.
There's contempt it can't disguise
In the little beady eyes
Of the spider sitting glowering in the bath.

It ignores my every lunge
With the back-brush and the sponge;
I have bombed it with 'A Present from Penarth';
But it doesn't mind at all—
It just rolls into a ball
And simply goes on squatting in the bath . . .

For hours we have been locked in endless struggle;
I have lured it to the deep end, by the drain;
At last I think I've washed it down the plug-'ole
But here it comes a-crawling up the chain!

Now it's time for me to shave
Though my nerves will not behave,
And there's bound to be a fearful aftermath;
So before I cut my throat
I shall leave this final note:
DRIVEN TO IT—BY THE SPIDER IN THE BATH!

co - bra to its lair, Killed a cro-co-dile ___ who dared to cross my path; But the
inch a-cross at least— It would frigh-ten e - ven Su -per-man or Garth. There's con-

thing I real-ly dread When I've just got out of bed Is to find that there's a spi - der in the
-tempt it can't dis-guise In the lit-tle bea-dy eyes Of the spi - der sit-ting glower-ing in the

bath.
bath.

I've no fear of wasps or bees, Mos -
It ig - nores my ev -ery lunge With the

- qui - tos on - ly tease, I ra - ther like a cri - cket on the hearth; But my
back-brush and the sponge; I have bombed it with 'A Pre-sent from Pen-arth'; But it

blood runs cold to meet In py - ja - mas and bare feet With a great big hai - ry spi - der in the
does -n't mind at all, It just rolls in -to a ball And sim - ply goes on squat-ting in the

bath. I have faced a char - ging bull in Bar - ce - lo - na, I have
bath. For hours we have been locked in end - less strug-gle; I have

dragged a moun-tain lio-ness from her cub, I've re -stored a mad go - ril - la to its
lured it to the deep end, by the drain; At last I think I've washed it down the

1.

rit.

ow - ner But I don't dare face that Tub... What a

192

plug-'ole (spoken) But here it comes a-crawling up the chain! Now it's

time for me to shave Though my nerves will not be-have, And there's bound to be a fear-ful af-ter-

-math; So be-fore I cut my throat I shall leave this fi-nal note: DRI-VEN

TO IT BY THE SPI-DER IN THE BATH!

The Warthog

The jungle was giving a party,
A post-hibernation ball,
The ballroom was crowded with waltzing gazelles,
Gorillas and zebras and all.
But who is that animal almost in tears
Pretending to powder her nose?
A poor little Warthog who sits by herself
In a pink satin dress with blue bows.
Again she is nobody's choice
And she sings in a sad little voice:

'No one ever wants to court a Warthog
Though a Warthog does her best;
I've spent a lot of money for a Warthog,
I am kiss-proofed, and prettily dressed.
I've lustre-rinsed my hair,
Dabbed perfume here and there,
My gums were tinted when I brushed my teeth;
   I'm young and in my prime
   But a wallflower all the time
   'Cause I'm a Warthog,
   Just a Warthog,
   I'm a Warthog underneath.'

Take your partners for a Ladies Excuse Me!

Excited and radiant she runs on the floor
To join the furore and fuss;
She taps on each shoulder and says, 'Excuse me',
And each couple replies, 'Excuse us!'
Then having no manners at all
They sing as they dance round the hall:

'No one ever wants to court a Warthog,
Though a Warthog does her best;
Her accessories are dazzling for a Warthog,
She is perfumed and daringly dressed.
We know her these and those
Are like Brigitte Bardot's,
Her gown is just a scintillating sheath,
    But she somehow fails to please
    'Cause everybody sees
    That she's a Warthog,
    Just a Warthog,
    She's a Warthog underneath!'

Head hanging, she wanders away from the floor,
This Warthog whom nobody loves,
Then stops in amazement, for there at the door
Stands a gentleman Warthog impeccably dressed
In the act of removing his gloves;
His fine chiselled face seems to frown
As he looks her first up and then down.

'I fancy you must be a sort of Warthog,
Though for a Warthog you look a mess.
That make-up's far too heavy for a Warthog;
You could have chosen a more suitable dress.
Did you have to dye your hair?
If that's perfume, give me air!
I strongly disapprove of scarlet teeth;
    But let us take the floor
    'Cause I'm absolutely sure
    That you're a Warthog,
    Just a Warthog,
    The sweetest little,
    Neatest little,
    Dearest and completest little
    Warthog . . . underneath!'

Fast waltz tempo ♩. = 68

1.The jun-gle was giv-ing a par-ty, A post-hi - ber-na - tion

ball, The ball-room was crowd-ed with waltz-ing ga - zelles, Go - ril - las and

rit. **Dolce: poco meno mosso** *p*

ze-bras and all. But

cant. *p*

Ped. *

196

who is that a-ni-mal al-most in tears Pre-tend-ing to pow-der her nose?

A poor lit-tle Wart-hog who sits by her-self In a pink sa-tin dress with blue

bows. _____ A-gain she is no-bo-dy's choice And she sings in a sad lit-tle

voice: _____

Moderato ♩. = 108

1. 'No one ev-er wants to court a Wart-hog, Though a
2. 'No one ev-er wants to court a Wart-hog, Though a

Wart - hog   does her best;   I've spent a lot of
Wart - hog   does her best;   Her ac - ces-so-ries   are

mo-ney for a Wart - hog,   I am kiss-proofed, and pret-ti - ly dressed.
daz-zling for a Wart - hog,   She is per - fumed and dar - ing-ly dressed.

I've lus - tre-rinsed my hair, ___ Dabbed per-fume here and there, ___ My
We know her these and those ___ Are like Bri-gitte Bar - dot's, ___ Her

gums were tin - ted when I brushed my teeth; ___   I'm young and in my
gown is just a scin - til - la - ting sheath, ___   But she some - how fails to

Ped.   *   Ped.   *

prime But a wall-flower all the time 'Cos I'm a Wart - hog,   Just a Wart - hog,
please   'Cos ev - 'ry bo - dy sees That she's a Wart - hog,   Just a Wart - hog,

I'm a   She's a   Wart - hog _____ un-der-neath!'

(spoken) Take your partners for a ladies' Excuse me!   Ex - ci -ted and

ra - diant she runs on the floor To join the fu - ro - re and fuss;   She

taps on each shoul-der and says, 'Ex-cuse me!' And each cou-ple re - plies, 'Excuse us!' *(spoken)*

Then hav-ing no man-ners at all They sing as they dance round the

Tempo 2 back to 𝄎 **|2. Tempo 3** *(Rather slower than Tempo 1)*

hall: ———— -neath!' Head hang-ing she

wan-ders a - way from the floor, This Wart-hog whom no-bo-dy loves, ——— Then

Faster quasi recit.

(spoken)

stops in amazement, for there at the door Stands a gen-tle-man Wart-hog im - pec-ca-bly

Dignified

dressed In the act of re - mov-ing his gloves; His fine chi-selled face seems to

Slower again

rit.

frown _____ As he looks her first up and then down. _____

Tempo I

(spoken)
'I fan - cy you must

be a sort of Wart - hog, Though for a Wart - hog you look a mess.

That make-up's far too hea - vy for a Wart - hog; You could have cho - sen

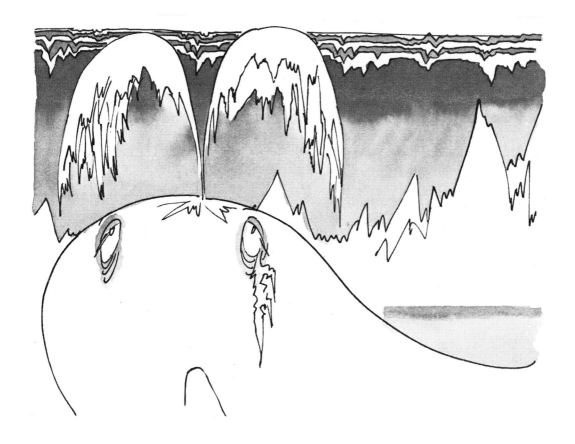

The Whale (Mopy Dick)

The bottle-nosed whale is a furlong long
And likewise wise but headstrong strong
And he sings this very lugubrious song
As he sails through the great Antarctic Ocean blue:

Oh, why do I swim through seas antarctical,
Freezing cold in every particle?
Some porpoises invited me to come and join their school;
They brought me here then swam away and shouted April Fool!
If ever I catch that school of porpoises
They won't get no Habeas Corpuses.
I'm lost and alone in a frozen zone
And I'm almost frozen too,
A shivering, quivering, bottle-nosed whale,
The bottle-nosed whale with the flu.

Oh, I used to play like a gay Leviathan
Squirting up jets like a soda siaphon;
Now every time I try to lift my hanky to my nose
A great harpoon goes whistling by, to a shout of
'There she blows!'

I like my oceans equatorial,
Where the water's warm, and the breeze less Boreal.
It's Fahrenheit minus twenty-nine, and I don't know what to do,
A rubbery, blubbery, bottle-nosed whale,
The bottle-nosed whale with the flu.

The bottle-nosed whale is a furlong long
And likewise wise but headstrong strong,
And he sings that very lugubrious song
As he sails through the ocean blue.

Though red your nose, though your toes are froze,
Though cold it seems to you,
Remember the tale of the bottle-nosed whale
Who has not even got his own hot water bot.,
The bottle-nosed whale with the flu!

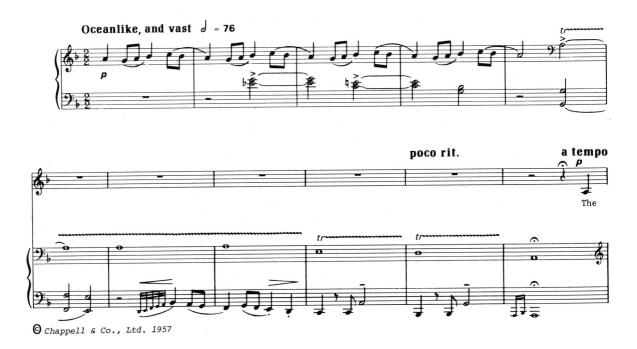

bot-tle-nosed whale is a fur-long long And like-wise wise but head-strong strong And he

sings this ve-ry lu - gu-brious song As he sails thro' the great Ant - arc - tic O - cean

poco rit. *ten.* **a tempo**

blue: Oh, why do I swim thro' seas ant - arc-ti-cal,

oo ———————— Freez-ing cold in ev - 'ry par-ti-cle? oo ——————

Some por-poi-ses in-vi-ted me to come and join their school; They

brought me here then swam a-way and shout-ed Ap-ril Fool.

If ev-er I catch that school of por-poi-ses oo ——————— They won't get no

Ha-be-as Cor-pus-es. oo——————— I'm lost and a-lone in a fro-zen zone and I'm

206

poco allarg.

al-most fro-zen too, A shi-ver-ing, qui-ver-ing, bot-tle-nosed whale, The bot-tle-nosed whale

rit. *(gasping wheeze)*

with the flu _____ ch, oo - ch

a tempo pesante

oo - ch oo - ah Tsch-oo _____ Oh, I used to play like a gay Le - vi-a-than

ugh huh huh huh ____ huh huh huh Squir-ting up jets like a so-da si-a-phon: Whoo - -

sf   *mf*   *mf*

8va bassa _ _ _ _ _ _ _ _ _ _ _ _

sf

-oosh! Now ev-ery time I try to lift my han-ky to my nose A great har-poon goes

whist-ling by, to a shout of 'There she blows!' ___

I like my o-ceans e-qua-to-ri-al, oo ___ Where the

wa-ter's warm, and the breeze less Bo-re-al. oo ___ It's Fah-ren-heit mi-nus

The Wild Boar

If you hear a loud *whoosh* in the African Bush
And an animal comes to the fore
Who is basically Pig, but more hairy and big,
You will know you have met with a Boar!
You are glued to the spot. Will he kill you or not?
No need to have fears about that;
Now he's made you stand fast and you're cornered at last,
All he wants is a Nice Little Chat.

But don't be misled. Soon you'll wish you were dead,
That instead he'd been after your gore—
For Oh! Oh! What a Bore he is,
What a thundering, thumping Boar!

In monotonous grunts he will tell you of hunts
Where for days he deluded the Field;
He will tell you his sow should be farrowing now
And enlarge on her annual yield;
He will say with an air that for brushing the hair
His bristle's the elegant thing,
And proudly confide they are after his hide
For no less a man than a King!

Then a joke he will try as you stifle a sigh
And deny that you've heard it before,
Thinking Oh! Oh! What a Bore he is,
What a thundering, thumping Boar!

As you laugh at his joke (ha-ha-ha) 'I'm a popular bloke,'
He will think, when you're ready to burst!
Then 'Hello there!' he'll cry to each poor passer-by—
The ones that have not seen him first!
For on sight of the beast, they will run to the east
And the north and the west and the south,
And long for the day when his head's on a tray
With a lemon to stop up his mouth!

They shout as they run: 'He's an excellent son
And a wonderful fellow, we're sure!
But Oh! Oh! What a Bore he is,
What a thundering, thumping,
Down in the dumping
Thumping Boar!'

Spikily ♩.= 96

1. If you hear a loud *whoosh* in the Af-ri-can bush And an an-im-al comes to the fore ____ Who is
2. In mo- -no-to-nous grunts he will tell you of hunts Where for days he de-lu-ded the Field; ____ He will

ba-si-cally pig, but more hai-ry and big, You will know you have met with a boar! (SNORT) You are
tell you his sow should be far-row-ing now And en-large on her an-nu-al yield; (SNORT) He will

213

glued to the spot. Will he kill you or not? No need to have fears a-bout that; Now he's
say with an air that for brush-ing the hair His bris-tle's the e - le-gant thing, And

poco meno mosso

made you stand fast and you're cor-nered at last, All he wants is a Nice Lit-tle Chat. But
proud-ly con-fide they are af - ter his hide For no less a man than the King! Then a

a tempo

don't be mis-led. Soon you'll wish you were dead, That in - stead he'd been af - ter your gore ___ For
joke he will try as you sti-fle a sigh And de - ny that you've heard it be - fore, ___ Think-ing

Ped.   Ped.

1.

Oh!   Oh! What a   Bore he is, What a   thun-der-ing, thump-ing   Boar! ___
Oh!   Oh! What a   Bore he is, What a   thun-der-ing, thump-ing

214

head's on a tray With a le-mon to stop up his mouth! They shout as they run: 'He's an

ex-cel-lent son and a won-der-ful fel-low, we're sure! _____ But Oh! Oh! what a

Bore he is! What a thun-der-ing, thump-ing down in the dump-ing

Thump-ing Boar.' _____ (SNORT)

216

The Wompom

You can do such a lot with a Wompom;
You can use every part of it too;
For work or for pleasure
It's a triumph, it's a treasure;
Oh, there's nothing that a Wompom cannot do!

Now the thread from the coat of a Wompom
Has the warmth and resilience of wool;
You need never wash or brush it,
It's impossible to crush it,
And it shimmers like the finest sort of tulle.

So our clothes are all made from the Wompom—
Model gowns, sportswear, lingerie—
They are waterproof and plastic,
Where it's needed they're elastic
And they emphasise the figure as you see.

        Hail to thee blithe Wompom,
        Hail to thee O plant,
        All providing Wompom,
        Universal Aunt!

You can shave with the rind of a Wompom
And it acts as a soapless shampoo,
And the root in little doses
Keeps you free from halitosis—
Oh, there's nothing that a Wompom cannot do!

217

Now the thick inner shell of a Wompom
You can mould with the finger and thumb;
Though soft when you began it
It will set as hard as granite
And it's quite as light as aluminium.

So we make what we like from the Wompom
And that proves very useful indeed;
From streets full of houses
To the buttons on your trousers,
With a Wompom you have everything you need.

> Gaudeamus Wompom,
> Gladly we salute
> Vademecum Wompom,
> Philanthropic fruit!

Oh the thin outer leaf of a Wompom
Makes the finest Havana cigar,
And its bottom simply bristles
With unusual looking thistles,
But we haven't yet discovered what they are!

You can do such a lot with a Wompom;
You can use every part of it too;
For work or for pleasure
It's a triumph, it's a treasure;
Oh, there's nothing that a Wompom cannot do!

Oh, the flesh in the heart of a Wompom
Has the flavour of Porterhouse Steak,
And the juice is a liquor
That will get you higher quicker—
And you're still lit up next morning when you wake!

> Wompom, Wompom,
> Let your voices ring,
> Wompom, Wompom,
> Evermore we sing!

To record *What is What* in a Wompom
Needs a book twice as big as *Who's Who*;
I could tell you more and more a-
Bout this fascinating flora:
You can shape it, you can square it,
You can drape it, you can wear it,
You can ice it, you can dice it,
You can pare it, you can slice it . . .
Oh, there's nothing that a Wompom cannot do!

218

Very lively ♩ = 168

FACTORY NOISES ad lib.

mf

1. You can do such a lot with a Wom-pom You can use ev-ery part of it too; for work and for plea-sure It's a tri-umph, it's a trea-sure; Oh, there's no-thing that a Wom-pom can-not do!

NOISES ad lib.

2. Now the

219

thread from the coat of a Wom-pom Has the warmth and re - si - lience of
(3.) clothes are all made from the Wom-pom Mo - del gowns, sports-wear, lin - - ge-
(6.) thick in - ner shell of a Wom-pom You can mould with the fin - ger and
(7.) make what we like from the Wom-pom And that proves ve - ry use-ful in -
(10.) do such a lot with a Wom-pom; You can use ev - ery part of it
(11.) flesh in the heart of a Wom-pom Has the fla - vour of Por-ter - house

wool; You need ne - ver wash or brush it, It's im - pos-si - ble to
-rie They are wa - ter-proof and plas-tic, Where it's need-ed they're e -
thumb; Though soft when you be - gan it It will set as hard as
-deed; From streets full of hous - es To the but-tons on your
too; For work or for plea-sure It's a tri - umph, it's a
Steak, And the juice is a li - quor That will get you high - er

Ped.   *   Ped.   *   Ped.   *

1. *(verses 2,6 and 10)*

crush it, And it shim-mers like the fi - nest sort of tulle.   3. So our
- las - tic And they em - pha - sise the fi - gure as you
gra - nite And it's quite as light as a - lu - mi - ni - um.   7. So we
trou-sers, With a Wom-pom you have ev - ery-thing you
trea-sure; Oh, there's no-thing that a Wom-pom can - not do!   11. Oh, the
qui-cker And you're still lit up next morn-ing when you

Ped.   *

2. *(verses 3,7 and 11)*   *(small notes last time only)*

(3.) see.   4. Hail   to   thee blithe   Wom - pom,   Hail   to
(7.) need.   8. Gau - de - a - mus   Wom - pom,   Glad - ly
(11.) wake!   12. Wom - - pom,   Wom - - pom,   Let   your

Ped.   *

thee O plant, _____ All pro-vi-ding Wom-pom,
we sa-lute _____ Va - de - me - cum Wom-pom,
voi - ces ring, _____ Wom - pom, Wom - pom,

U - ni - ver - sal Aunt! 5. You can shave with the rind of a Wom-pom
Phi - lan-thro-pic fruit! 9. Oh the thin ou-ter leaf of a Wom-pom
Ev - er - more we sing! 13. To re-cord *What is What* in a Wom-pom

And it acts as a soap-less sham-poo, And the root in lit-tle
Makes the fi - nest Ha - va-na ci - gar, And its bot-tom sim-ply
Needs a book twice as big as *Who's Who*; I could tell you more and

Ped. ❋ Ped. ❋

1.
(verses 5 and 9)

do - ses Keeps you free from ha - li - to-sis Oh, there's no-thing that a Wom-pom can-not
bris-tles With un - u-sual-look-ing this-tles, But we have-n't yet dis - co-vered what they
more a - bout this fa - sci - na - ting flo-ra: You can

221

Afterword

(This unpublished verse was completed by Michael Flanders sometime in 1974)

I was born at 04 hundred hours on 1/3/22
Somerset House was notified
'A little 7874322 (Column 159)'.
Baptism later certified
(Parish Register Page 183):
'I name this child . . . 1242'.

Our family lived variously at 33 N.W.8
73 N.W.8, 1 and 9 N.W.11
And gloriously, for a while, in a country cottage
National Grid reference TQ 7024 (correct to one kilometre)

I passed my schooldays without much sense of identity
(Post Office Savings Book 1990 A)
In Lower and Upper 4ths and 5ths and 6ths
(Locker No 23)
Was 12th man in the 1st Eleven and rowed 7 in the Eight.

September 3rd, 1939 I was identified BIA 1526045;
1941—A. B. RNVR Red Division Starboard Watch
PJX 276123

And here I am
Stamped sealed and delivered

Passport No. 77922 F.O. London 23/2/66
National Insurance ZB 88 81 17B
Driving Licence 5Z/107206
Telephone Number 01 –983– Double 747
To my doctor: BIA 1526045
To my Banker: 37705873
To my Union: B 16776

V.A.T. 223 3859 66 . . .

And TIME LIFE International (Amsterdam) Inc. addresses me as
Mr Flanders 581 101 L03 FLAN—063 M 992 but refers to me in
private as 400000 00840 0 1 00183N 06 S 29.

My days are numbered.